'You're like twins [...] other.'

'We don't want to. We have to.'

'I wonder.' Razin, a Ukrainian with a furrowed smile and wary eyes who had been ordered to protect Antonov, rolled the creased cardboard tube of his yellow cigarette between thumb and forefinger. 'Are you sure you don't want to kill him?'

Antonov considered the question carefully. When he hunted animals – deer, elk, lynx – yes, he wanted to kill; that was sport and it was senseless to deny its pleasures. But to want to kill a man, no. Antonov shook his head vigorously. That was duty. 'I'm sure,' he told the Ukrainian.

'Maybe *he* wants to kill *you*.'

Vendetta

by

Derek Lambert

SPHERE BOOKS LIMITED

SPHERE BOOKS LTD

Published by the Penguin Group
27 Wrights Lane, London W8 5TZ, England
Viking Penguin Inc., 40 West 23rd Street, New York, New York 10010, USA
Penguin Books Canada Ltd, 2801 John Street, Markham, Ontario, Canada L3R 1B4
Penguin Books (NZ) Ltd, 182–190 Wairau Road, Auckland 10, New Zealand

Penguin Books Ltd, Registered Offices: Harmondsworth, Middlesex, England

First published in Great Britain by Hamish Hamilton Ltd 1986
Published by Sphere Books Ltd 1988

Printed and bound in Great Britain by
Richard Clay Ltd, Bungay, Suffolk

For Jack and Nora, good neighbours

I am tired and sick of war. Its glory is all moonshine . . . War is hell.

Attributed to General Sherman in an address at Michigan University on June 19, 1879.

AUTHOR'S NOTE

In 1942 while savage fighting was at its height in Stalingrad two snipers, one Russian and one German, stalked each other among the ruins. In this prolonged duel within a battle each marksman became the embodiment of his country's desperate designs. That much is fact; in the rest of the book, historical detail apart, the only truth is hope.

CHAPTER ONE

The young man cleaning his gun smelled cold, the true cold that is a prelude to snow, and was comforted. Snow was the white crib of security before the Army took him.

He peered over the rim of the shell-crater. To the east, across the Volga, beyond the smoke and dust of battle, the grey October sky was metallic-bright, but the breath of winter was unmistakable.

To a Siberian, that is.

Razin pulled him down to the planks laid in a square around the stove. 'Have you gone crazy? Why don't you do the job properly, stick a wreath on your helmet?'

'He couldn't see me.' Antonov picked up his rifle and with a rag massaged yellow oil into the stock beneath the telescopic sight.

'Couldn't see you?' Razin took a crumpled pack of *papirosy* from his faded brown tunic, squatted beside the stove and lit one from its flanks; specks of tobacco sparked and died on the glowing metal. 'You have his eyes?'

'There's no cover for him out there.' Antonov jerked his thumb in the direction of the mangled rail tracks, known to the Germans as the Tennis Racquet, separating the river from the tooth-stump ruins of Stalingrad.

Katyusha mortar rockets fired from the far bank of the Volga exploded in German-held rubble. A German field gun replied. Antonov longed for the snow-silence of the steppe or

1

its stunned summer stillness or the breathing quiet of its nights.

'And I suppose you know what he's doing?' Razin, an old soldier of twenty-eight, pulled at the ragged droop of his moustache and pushed his steel helmet onto the back of his cropped hair.

'Eating probably. It's lunchtime. Sausage? Bread? Maybe an apple if he's lucky.' Antonov removed a flake of ash from Razin's cigarette from the barrel of the Mosin-Nagant.

'Beer? Schnapps?'

'No liquor. He needs a steady hand.'

'Like you?'

'Like me,' Antonov agreed.

'And he knows what you're doing?'

'If he were asked he'd probably answer: "Cleaning his gun." It's a good bet.'

'You're like twins and yet you want to kill each other.'

'We don't want to. We have to.'

'I wonder.' Razin, a Ukrainian with a furrowed smile and wary eyes who had been ordered to protect Antonov, rolled the creased cardboard tube of his yellow cigarette between thumb and forefinger. 'Are you sure you don't want to kill him?'

Antonov considered the question carefully. When he hunted animals – deer, elk, lynx – yes, he wanted to kill; that was sport and it was senseless to deny its pleasures. But to want to kill a man, no. Antonov shook his head vigorously. That was duty. 'I'm sure,' he told the Ukrainian.

'You shook your head as if you wanted to get rid of your brains. A little too energetically, comrade?'

'Meister's special. Maybe that's why I over-react.'

'And the other Fritzes you killed . . . Weren't they special to their parents, wives, girls?'

Antonov who had shot and killed twenty-three Germans since he arrived in Stalingrad three weeks earlier, each with one bullet, said: 'You know what I mean.'

'Maybe *he* wants to kill *you*.'

Did he? Antonov doubted it: Meister, with his special

2

talents, was merely serving his country. Like me. Hitler instead of Stalin. It wasn't until he had been ordered to kill Meister that it had occurred to him that the motives of enemies could be the same. The knowledge worried him. He placed his rifle on a plank, covering the sights with the rag.

A machine-gun coughed nearby and two soldiers jumped into the shell-hole. Razin cocked his pistol because when the enemy lines were only a couple of hundred metres away, when positions could be captured and recaptured within minutes, it was wise to check out visitors. They were both young, Slav faces smudged with exhaustion. One of them tugged a flask from his tunic, took a swig of vodka from it and passed it around. Russia's fuel, Antonov thought. Where would we be without it?

'You don't drink firewater?' The owner of the flask looked astonished.

'When did you last eat?' Antonov always tried to redirect attention from his abstinence.

'Eat?' The second soldier, once-plump cheeks sagging into pouches, used his hands like an actor. 'This year perhaps: I can't remember. When did we last eat, Sergei?'

'I don't know but these two look well fed.' He touched a blood-stained bandage above his knee-length boot. 'Why so glossy, comrades? Dead men's rations?'

Razin, offering his cigarettes, said: 'We're privileged. In a classless society there'll always be some of us. Or hadn't you noticed?'

'Are you political?'

'You know better than that. Military commissars had their teeth drawn on October the ninth on the Boss's orders.'

True, but Antonov could understand the soldier's suspicion: although the commissars' powers had been curtailed to reduce friction in the army, NKVD units were posted on the west bank of the Volga to stop the faint-hearted escaping to the safety of the east.

Was Razin in any way political? Antonov doubted it. During their brief but congested relationship Razin had emerged as an escapist, a stunted intellectual who had sought

3

refuge from responsibility in the army.

Antonov reached into an ammunition box containing black bread, an onion, cheese and raw fish blown out of the Volga with hand-grenades.

The soldier with the pouched cheeks spoke to his colleague with his hand. 'Careful,' the hand said with a loose-wristed shake. 'These men could be dangerous.' But he took the food, pulling it apart with his fingers and handing the larger portion to his partner. They ate ravenously.

The machine-gun opened up again, a longer burst this time, welded explosions like ripping calico. More Katyushas. An aching pause. Then the cries of wounded men.

Razin swigged from the flask. 'Good stuff.' He wiped his mouth with the back of his hand.

'The best,' the soldier with the wounded leg agreed. 'Ahot-nichaya, hunters' vodka.'

The cries of the wounded faded without arousing comment in the shell-hole. Suffering had become unremarkable and yet one soldier would still give another the larger of two crusts of bread. There were many values among the soldiery that puzzled Antonov. Indeed from the beginning it had been the relationships between men at war rather than the cannonade of battle that had disturbed him most. He found it difficult to share with them.

Hunger satisfied, the once-plump soldier became wary again; he reminded Antonov of a Bolshevik during the Revolution interrogating a prisoner suspected of Czarist sympathies, truculence tempered by grudging deference. 'So,' the soldier said, 'where have you two been fighting? In the cookhouse?'

'Nowhere much,' Razin told him. 'I was with the 258th Rifle Division in a small skirmish – the Battle of Moscow. Were you there?'

'Rostov.'

'Ah yes,' Razin said. 'You lost Rostov: we saved Moscow.'

'We heard that when you saved Moscow the war was as good as over. What went wrong?'

The other soldier said: 'Rostov was a victory,' and when

4

Razin laughed: 'I mean it, Rostov was the turning point. It was after Rostov that Stalin said: "Not a step back."'

'And we haven't taken any steps back?'

'We'll hold the bastards here. Stalingrad. This is the one.'

Razin, nipping the glowing tip off his cigarette and, pouring the residue of tobacco into a tin that had contained throat lozenges, said: 'I was in Moscow when Panfilov's men held the Fritzes.'

The two soldiers fell silent as Razin retold the story that had already acquired the lustre of a legend.

As the German offensive faltered outside Moscow in late 1941, nearly a year ago, twenty-eight anti-tank gunners commanded by an officer named Panfilov had defied the mailed fist of a panzer attack on the Volokolamsk Highway. They had fought with guns and grenades and petrol bombs and the political officer, mortally wounded, had grabbed a clutch of hand grenades and thrown himself under a German tank. The battle had lasted four hours. The Germans lost eighteen tanks and failed to break through.

Ah, such sacrifice. Even when Razin had finished the tale *Rodina*, Mother Russia, lingered in the crater and briefly Panfilov and his men with their petrol-filled bottles were more real than the outrage that was Stalingrad.

Razin said: 'At the end of the battle for Moscow you couldn't help feeling sorry for the Fritzes. It was so cold that the oil in their guns froze and the poor bastards were still wearing summer uniforms – greatcoats and boots if they were lucky – and when they went for a piss . . . snap!' Razin picked up a splinter of wood and snapped it in half.

'You felt sorry for the parasites?' The soldier with the eloquent hands stared at Razin in disbelief.

'Until I remembered what they had done to our people. Until I remembered the corpses strung up in the villages.'

'The Fritzes might have been pissing icicles at Moscow,' the soldier with the wounded leg remarked, 'but when they first arrived in Stalingrad they were singing and playing mouth-organs.' He turned to Antonov. 'You don't talk much, comrade. What do you think about Germans? Do you feel

5

sorry for them?'

Antonov realised that the soldier thought he might be a Nazi sympathiser: the Red Army was obsessed with spies, and exhausted men saw them on the tattered fringes of their fatigue. But Antonov wasn't sure what he felt about Germans. Occasionally during shell-splintered sleep, he saw young men harvesting golden wheat on the steppe or carving ice for drinking water from a frozen river or coaxing girls into the deep green depths of the taiga and the young men were neither Russians nor Germans.

When Antonov didn't reply the other soldier, wagging one finger, asked: 'Where are you from comrade? The Ukraine? I heard that when the Fritzes invaded last year a lot of Ukrainians fought for them.'

Razin prodded the barrel of his pistol towards the soldier. 'I come from the Ukraine,' he said.

'You obviously decided to fight on the right side.' The soldier regarded the pistol without fear. 'But what I'm saying is true?'

'A few joined the Germans,' Razin admitted. 'In Kiev, for instance, the people were bewildered. In the space of twenty years they had been occupied by Germans, Austrians, Reds, Whites, Poles . . . Maybe all they wanted was the use of their own backyard. And isn't that what we're all fighting for? One hell of a great backyard?'

The other soldier spread his hands in front of the incandescent stove. 'That isn't what Sergei asked. Where,' nodding at Antonov, 'do you come from?'

More Katyushas, Little Kates, exploded nearby. They made an awesome noise and the Germans called them Stalin Organs. For the Russians firing from the other side of the Volga it was easy enough to shell the Germans over their comrades' heads; for the Germans it wasn't so easy to pound the Russians because the Soviet positions were so compressed that there was always a risk that they would hit their own infantry.

'Does it matter? We're all Soviets.' But to Antonov it did matter; the army had taught him that. Republics, regions,

6

races . . . all harboured ancient hostilities.

The wounded soldier said: 'A country boy by the look of you. Blue eyes, fair hair beneath that helmet . . . Or is it straw?'

Antonov drew a swastika on the dust on one of his tall boots. 'Siberia,' he said after a while. 'A village near Novosibirsk.'

In fact it was fifty miles away from the city, a collection of wooden cottages with pink and blue fretted eaves, a pump and a wooden church that was used as a granary.

'Well,' the wounded soldier said, 'you look as if you've had an easy war so far.'

Razin said: 'Very easy. He's only shot twenty-three so far. Two more won't make much difference.' He smiled crookedly at the two soldiers.

They began to understand, expressions tightening. 'You're not – '

Removing the rag from the telescopic sights of his rifle, Antonov said: 'My name's Yury Antonov,' and, without pleasure, observed the effect of his name on the two visitors.

CHAPTER TWO

Leaning against the belly of a stricken locomotive, Karl Meister ate his lunch. Stale bread, sausage and a can of sliced peaches.

He wondered what Antonov was doing. Cleaning his rifle probably. If you weren't eating or sleeping or shooting you were cleaning your rifle.

Katyushas exploded down the ruptured track near Univermag, the department store. They sounded like elephants bellowing. Fragments of metal struck the other side of the big black engine.

Cold eased its way down from the north. No teeth to it yet but when it really began its advance – next month according to the pundits – it would be inexorable. More than anything else the Sixth Army feared the cold: it had bitten the Wehrmacht to pieces outside Moscow.

Feeling its breath, Corporal Ernst Lanz, a thirty-year-old Berliner with a bald patch and a thief's face, said: 'We were supposed to have gobbled up this *arschloch* of a place in August.'

He was leaning against a piston drinking Russian beer from a fluted brown bottle. His grey-green tunic was stained but the Iron Cross 1st class on his chest shone brightly. His helmet, upturned, lay beside him like a bucket.

'The generals didn't reckon with street fighters,' Meister said. 'The Ivans would fight for a blade of grass – if there was

8

any left.'

'Stalingrad!' Lanz threw aside the empty bottle. 'Six months ago I'd never heard of it.'

'I doubt whether the Führer had. No one expected a battle here. We thought we'd be half way across Siberia: the Russians thought they would be across the Dneiper.'

In Lanz's presence Meister tried to compensate for his lack of battle experience with tactical hindsight and foresight. He doubted whether either was effective: not even shared adversity could dispel the suspicions separating classes: all they had in common was a city upbringing and even that was marred by Lanz's low opinion of Hamburg.

He wondered how, given a common tongue, he and Antonov would hit it off if they hadn't been ordered to kill each other. According to Soviet propaganda Antonov was the son of the soil, a Siberian. Would he want to socialise with a college boy?

'So,' Lanz said, taking a cigarette from a looted silver case and lighting it, 'when are you going to start hunting each other again? What is this? A rest period?'

Meister swallowed the last slippery segment of peach. 'When I'm ready,' he said.

'Supposing he gets ready first? Gets a bead on you from over there,' pointing towards what was left of a warehouse.

'He won't, he's not stupid, he knows I'd see him first silhouetted against the sky.'

'That's what you call instinct?'

'Antonov has instinct. He was a hunter. I have aptitude.'

Aptitude, substitute for talent. Squinting through the sights of a Karabiner 98K on the college rifle range because he knew he could never excel at sport. Muscular co-ordination, that was what he had lacked but when it came to punching bullseyes with bullets he knew no equal and when he became a crack shot he had as many girls flirting with him as any lithe-limbed athlete, one girl in particular, Elzbeth, who had blonde hair like spun glass. He kept a photograph of her in his wallet, posing with him in Berlin when he won the Cadet Marksman of the Year award, he with his black hair glossy in

9

the flashlights smiling fiercely over the rim of the enormous cup. Elzbeth said his face was sensitive. Some qualification for a sniper!

Lanz drew on his cigarette, cupped in his hand convict fashion. 'Instinct versus aptitude . . . Which will win?'

'You'd better pray for aptitude. If I lose, you lose and there's no place in the Third Reich for losers.'

'Don't worry about me,' Lanz said. 'I'm a survivor. And if you want to survive take a few tips from me; that's why we're partners. Remember?'

'I remember,' Meister said.

'So make your move when we launch the next attack on Mamaev Hill.' They had lost count of how many times the hill commanding Stalingrad had changed hands. At the moment it was shared, a pyramid of rubble, exploded shells and corpses, some not quite dead. 'You'll have good cover. Smoke, shell-bursts. Tanks – T-34s or Panthers.'

Which, Meister thought, is exactly what Antonov will be anticipating. I might not know the arts of survival in battle but in this lone game I am Lanz's master.

'You don't agree?' Lanz asked.

'It's a possibility.'

'I didn't ask for this job.'

'I couldn't have done it without you. Survived this.' Meister gestured at the desolation that had been a city.

'When you've been running from the cops all your life you know a trick or two.'

'Did you have any trouble getting into the Army? You know, with your record . . . '

'I'm not a Jew, I'm not a gypsy. It was easy.'

'But why' Meister asked curiously, 'did you want to fight?'

'Who said I did? The Kripo had other plans for me if I didn't.' Lanz ground out his cigarette end and rubbed his bald patch with his hand leaving behind a grey smudge. 'And you? Weren't you too young to be conscripted?'

Meister who was now eighteen said: 'I volunteered.'

A shelf of trophies, a head full of golden words. For the Fatherland. For the Führer. For Elzbeth.

10

'Are you scared of dying?' Lanz asked.

'Aren't we all?'

'Some people beckon death. They call them heroes. Others dispatch people to their deaths. They call them politicians. But you haven't answered my question.'

A Stuka dropped out of the sky, bent wings predatory, its pilot looking for Russians burrowing in the ruins, or ships crossing the Volga. An anti-aircraft gun opened up on the other side of the river.

'I don't want to die,' Meister said.

'Then you *must* kill Antonov.'

'Of course.' He saw Antonov with a ploughshare, its blades turning furrows of wet black earth.

A scout car stopped beside the stricken engine and a young officer with bloodshot eyes climbed out. 'Are you Meister?'

Meister said he was.

'The general wants to see you.'

'*The* general?'

'General Friedrich von Paulus.' The officer looked as incredulous as Meister felt.

***

Paulus, commander of the Sixth Army that was laying siege to Stalingrad, sat at a trestle table beneath a naked light bulb in a command post, a cellar to the west of the city, poring over two maps. He didn't look up when Meister clattered down the stone steps.

The larger map embraced the southern front. Meister could see the arrow-heads of Army Group A piercing the Caucasus, probing for its oil; above them the arrows of Army Group B trying to cut the Russians' artery, the Volga, and amputate the great thumb of land that linked the Soviet Union with Turkey and Iran.

But the arrows lost direction at Stalingrad, the once prosperous city of half a million inhabitants. Stalingrad was the smaller map and, standing to attention opposite Paulus, Meister was able to view the plan of battle from the Soviet

11

positions on the east bank of the Volga.

The plight of the Russians became more apparent in the cellar than it did above ground. Stalingrad was on the west bank and the Soviet forces there were encircled and divided. They were ferociously defending the industrial north and their slender waterside footholds, but nine-tenths of the city was in German hands.

At last the general leaned back in his chair and looked at Meister. Paulus had a long handsome face and big ears and his dark hair had been pressed close to his scalp by the peaked cap lying on the table. His uniform was loose on his body but he had presence. He was smoking a cigarette and there was a mound of crushed butts on a saucer.

'So,' he said, 'you're our latest hero.' He appraised Meister as though looking for a hidden feature. 'Well, we could do with one. Stand at ease, man.' He picked up a copy of *Signal*. 'Have you seen this?' handing Meister the forces' magazine.

'No, Herr General.' Meister found it difficult to believe that he was alone in a cellar with a general. He riffled the pages of the magazine until he saw Elzbeth and himself. It was the same photograph that he carried in his wallet.

'Keep it,' Paulus said. 'Read it later. Don't worry, it's very flattering. I understand from Berlin that most of the newspapers have picked up the story. You, Meister, are just the tonic the German people need. They've been reading too much lately about "heavy fighting". They know by now what that means – a setback. And do you know what that makes you?'

'No, Herr General.'

A shell exploded nearby. The cellar trembled, the lightbulb swung.

'A diversionary tactic.' Paulus pulled at one of his big ears and lit another cigarette. 'A sideshow. But at the moment the German people don't know about your co-star.'

'Antonov?' Meister's throat tickled; it was a sniper's nightmare to cough or sneeze as, target in the sights, he caressed the trigger of his rifle.

'So far this rivalry – this feud within a battle – has been for

12

local consumption. But not when you kill him.'

Meister cleared his throat but the tickle remained.

'Then,' Paulus said, 'the whole Fatherland will know about Karl Meister's greatest exploit. It will be symbolic, the victory of National Socialist over Bolshevism.'

The irritation scratched at Meister's throat. Any minute now he would be racked with coughs.

Paulus unbuttoned the top pocket of his tunic. 'I have a message for you. It's from the Führer.' Paulus read from a folded sheet of paper. *'I have heard about the exploits of Karl Meister and I am profoundly moved by both his dedication and his expertise. I am led to understand that the Bolsheviks, having forcibly been made aware of Meister's accomplishments, have produced a competitor. I confidently await your communiqué to the effect that Meister has disposed of him.'*

Meister said: 'Antonov is very good.' He tried unsuccessfully to dislodge the irritation in his throat with one rasping cough.

'But not as good as you?'

'I'm not sure. He comes from the country, I come from a city, Hamburg. Maybe I have the edge, city sharpness . . . But he has instinct, a hunter's instinct.'

Paulus said: 'You are better. The Führer knows this,' in a tone that was difficult to identify.

'With respect, General Paulus,' Meister said, 'I think we are equal. I think he and I know that.' He coughed again.

'Know? You have some sort of communication?'

'Respect,' Meister said.

'How many Russians have you killed?'

Meister who knew Paulus knew said: 'Twenty-three. According to the Soviet propaganda Antonov has killed twenty-three Germans.'

Paulus said: 'Do you *want* to kill him?' and Meister, still trying to blunt the prickles in his throat, said: 'Of course, because if I don't he will kill me.'

'Tell me, Meister, what makes you so different? What makes a sniper? A good eye, a steady hand . . . thousands of men have these qualifications.'

13

'Anticipation, Herr General.' Meister wasn't sure. A flash of sunlight on metal, a fall of earth, a crack of a breaking twig . . . such things helped but there was more, much more. You had to know your adversary.

'And Antonov has this same quality?'

'Without a doubt. That's what makes him so good.'

He saw Antonov and himself as skeletons stripped of predictability. Anticipating anticipation.

He began to cough. The sharp coughs sounded theatrical but he couldn't control them. He heard Paulus say: 'I hope you don't cough like that when you've got Antonov in your sights. Are you sick?' when he had finished.

'Just nerves,' Meister said.

Losing interest in the cough, Paulus, leaning forward, said: 'So, what are your impressions of the battle, young man?'

Handling his words with care, Meister told Paulus that he hadn't expected the fighting to be so prolonged, so concentrated.

Paulus, speaking so softly that Meister could barely hear him, said: 'Nor did I.' He stared at the arrows on the maps. 'Do you have any theories about the name of this God-forsaken place?'

'Stalingrad? I've heard that Stalin is determined not to lose the city named after him.'

'Stalin was here in 1918,' Paulus said. 'During the Civil War when it was called Tsaritsyn. The Bolsheviks sent the White Guards packing just about now, October. Stalin took a lot of the credit for it.' Paulus leaned back from his maps. 'Have you heard anyone suggest that the Führer is determined to capture Stalingrad because of its name?'

'No, Herr General,' Meister lied. He had but he didn't believe it.

Paulus asked: 'Have you ever considered the possibility of defeat, Meister?'

'Never.'

'Good.' With one finger Paulus deployed his troops on the smaller of the two maps. 'We didn't expect the Russians to fight so fanatically.' He seemed to be thinking aloud. When

14

he looked up his face was drained by his thoughts. He waved one hand. 'Very well, Meister, you may go. Good luck.'

'One question, Herr General?'

Paulus inclined his head.

'Wouldn't it be better if the people back home knew about Antonov now? It would be a better story, the rivalry between the two of us.'

'They will,' Paulus said.

'Why not now?'

'I should have thought that was obvious,' Paulus said. 'In case Antonov kills you first.'

Meister began to cough again.

CHAPTER THREE

At dawn on the following day Meister went looking for Antonov.

During the night, frost had crusted the mud, and rimed the ruins so that, with mist rising from the Volga, they had an air of permanency about them, relics from some medieval havoc. Among the relics soldiers roused themselves to continue the business of killing, moving lethargically like a yawning new day-shift. It was a time for snipers.

Lanz walked ahead of Meister, rifle in one hand, sketch map in the other, as they left the remains of the Central railway station where they had spent the night after the interview with Paulus. The prolonged meeting had made it unnecessary for Meister to even consider Lanz's advice to stalk Antonov during the assault on Mamaev Hill: the attack had taken place and for the time being it was in German hands.

Lanz's map supposedly indicated safe streets but in Stalingrad in October, 1942, there were no such thoroughfares: even now survivors of Rodimtsev's tall guardsmen and Batyuk's root-chewing Mongols lurked among the relics.

They turned into a street that had been lined with wooden houses. Although they had been destroyed in August when 600 German bombers had attacked the city killing, so it was said, more than 30,000 civilians, you could still smell fire.

Corpses lying among the charred timber were crystallised with frost.

Lanz, who was slightly bow-legged, paused beneath a leafless plane tree and said: 'What's it like to have a personal minesweeper?'

'What's it like to have a personal marksman?'

But of the two of them Lanz was the true protector: Lanz took the broad view of battle, Meister viewed it through his sights. Meister thought that Lanz, peering from beneath his steel helmet, looked like a tortoise.

'Time for breakfast?' Lanz asked.

'When we get to the square,' mildly surprised to hear himself, a soldier as raw as a grazed knuckle, giving orders to a corporal.

The bullet smacked into the flaking trunk of the tree above Meister's head. He and Lanz hit the ground.

After a few seconds Lanz said: 'Antonov?'

'Antonov wouldn't have missed.'

Holding his rifle, a Karabiner 98K fitted with a ZF 41 telescopic sight, Meister edged behind the bole of the tree to wait for the second shot.

The marksman, amateurish or, perhaps, wounded, was firing from the wreckage of a wooden church across the street. The fallen dome lay in the nave, a giant mushroom.

Meister, peering through his sights, looked for the sniper's cover. If I were him . . . the altar just visible past the dome. He steadied the rifle, disciplined his breathing, took first pressure on the trigger.

River-smelling mist drifted along the street but it was thinning.

The second shot spat frozen mud into Lanz's face. The marksman, whose fur hat had risen in Meister's sights, reared and fell behind the altar.

'Twenty-four,' Lanz said.

They ate breakfast in a cellar in Ninth of January Square where in September Sergeant Pavlov and sixty men barricaded in a tall house had held up the German tanks for a week.

17

They ate bread and cheese and drank ersatz coffee handed over reluctantly by a group of soldiers when Lanz showed them a chit signed by the commanding officer of the 3rd Battalion, 194th Infantry Regiment, to which Meister was attached.

The infantrymen looked very young and they were trying to look tough; instead they looked bewildered and Meister felt much older and decided that it was his singleness of purpose, his detachment from the overall battle, that made this so.

One of them, eighteen or so with smooth cheeks and soft stubble on his chin, said: 'So you're Meister. What makes you tick?' his accent Bavarian, and another, leaner faced, with a northern intonation: 'They say you've killed 23 Ivans. True, or is it propaganda?'

Lanz answered him. 'Correction. Twenty-four. He just killed one round the corner,' making it sound as though Meister had won a game of skat.

'I don't know what makes me tick,' Meister said to the Bavarian.

'Do you enjoy killing Russians?'

'I do my job.'

'What sort of answer is that?'

'Do *you* enjoy what you're doing?'

'Are you crazy?' the northerner asked. 'Before I came to Russia I'd never even heard of Stalingrad. It's like fighting on the moon.'

Meister drank some bitter coffee. His mother had made beautiful coffee and in the mornings its breakfast smell had reached his bedroom and when he had opened his window he had smelled pastries from the elegant patisserie next door, a refreshing change from the smell of perfume from his father's factory that permeated the elegant house in Hamburg.

'What's it like being a hero?' the Bavarian asked.

'Great,' Lanz answered.

'I suppose you'll get an Iron Cross if you kill Antonov,' the Bavarian said ignoring Lanz. 'And a commission and a reception in the Adlon Hotel in Berlin.'

'*If* I kill him,' Meister said. 'But in any case I don't want any

18

of those things,' and Lanz said: 'How do you know about the Adlon?'

'I've been around,' the Bavarian said. He produced a looted bottle of vodka from his tunic and poured some down his throat. 'Great stuff. Better than schnapps.' He choked and turned away.

'Come on,' Lanz said to Meister, 'move yourself – you've got an appointment with Comrade Antonov.'

'Look out for mines,' the northerner warned them. 'We've been using dogs to explode them. The lieutenant lost his Dobermann that way. Where are you going anyway?'

'Mamaev Hill,' Meister told him.

'Shit. Are you sure it's ours? It could have changed hands again – the Russians shipped a lot of troops across the river in the mist.'

'Then Antonov will be early for his appointment,' Lanz said.

***

By 10 am the frost had melted and the mist had lifted and galleons of white cloud sailed serenely in the autumn-blue sky above Mamaev Hill which was still in German hands.

From a shell-hole on the hill, once a Tartar burial ground, more recently a picnic area, now a burial ground again, Meister could see the industrial north of Stalingrad and, to the south, the commercial and residential quarter. And he could make out the shape of the city, a knotted rope, twenty or more miles long, braiding this, the west bank of the Volga. It was rumoured that the German High Command hadn't anticipated such an elastic sprawl; nor, it was said, had they envisaged such a breadth of water, splintered with islands and creeks.

Through his field-glasses he could see the Russian heavy artillery and the eight and twelve-barrelled Katyusha launchers spiking the fields and scrub pine on the far bank. He scanned the river, clear today of timber and bodies because, although they had used flares, the German gunners hadn't been able to see the Russian relief ships in the mist-choked night.

Where was Antonov?

Meister swung the field-glasses to the north where only factory chimneys remained intact, fingers prodding the sky. He wouldn't be there: snipers don't prosper in hand-to-hand fighting.

He looked south. To the remnants of the State Bank, the brewery, the House of Specialists, Gorki Theatre. No, Antonov would be nearer to the hill than that, moving cautiously towards Mamaev, Stalingrad's principal vantage point. Scanning it with his field-glasses . . .

Meister shrank into the shell-hole. Lanz handed him pale coffee in a battered mess tin. 'Where is he?'

'Down there.' Meister pointed towards the river bank. 'Somewhere near Crossing 62. In No Man's Land.'

'Will you be able to get a shot at him?'

'Not a chance. He won't show himself, not while I'm up here.'

'He knows you're here?'

'He would be up here if the Russians still held Mamaev. It's the only place where you can see how the battle's going. Who's holding the vantage points.'

'You'll be a general one day,' Lanz said.

'I wanted to be an architect.'

'I want to rob the Reichsbank. Instead I became a nanny.'

Meister, who was never quite sure how to handle Lanz in this mood, drank the rest of his foul coffee. It was said to be made from acorns and dandelion roots and there was no reason to contest this.

Lanz lay back on the sloping bank of the crater, lit a cigarette and said: 'How long is this going to last?' words emerging in small billows of smoke.

'Antonov and me? God knows. It's been official for three days thanks to *Red Star*.'

If the Soviet army newspaper hadn't matched Antonov against him the duel would never have started.

A Yak, red stars blood-bright on its tail and fuselage, flew low overhead. The Germans held the two airfields, Gumrak and Pitomik, but the Russians held the whole of Siberia. They could retreat forever, Meister thought.

'I wish to hell it was over,' Lanz said.

'One way or the other?'

Lanz, smoking hungrily, didn't reply.

Meister thought: 'What would I be doing now if I were Antonov?' and knew immediately. He would be checking whether any Russians had been killed today by a single marksman's shot.

Could he find out about the sniper who had died at the altar near Ninth of January Square? Russians isolated in pockets of resistance were often in radio contact with Red Army headquarters.

Yes, it was possible.

CHAPTER FOUR

Yury Antonov, waiting for Razin to return from a command post, dozed in a tunnel leading to the river.

He saw sunflowers with blossoms like smiling suns crayoned by children and he heard the insect buzz from the taiga shouldering the wheatfields and he smelled the red polish that his mother used in the wooden cottage.

It had been a languorous Sunday early in September when they had come for him. He had been lying fully clothed on his bed picturing the naked breasts of a girl named Tasya who lived in the next village. His younger brother, Alexander, was sitting on the verandah drinking tea with his father and his mother was in the kitchen feeding the bowl of borsch bubbling on the stove.

After a Komsomol meeting the previous evening he had walked Tasya home. He had kissed her awkwardly, feeling the gentle thrust of her breasts against his chest, and ever since had been perturbed by the intrusion of lascivious images into the purity of his love.

He was almost eighteen, exempt from military service because of a heart murmur triggered by rheumatic fever, and she was seventeen. He was worried that, like other girls, she might be intoxicated by the glamour of the other young men departing to fight the Germans. A farm labourer wasn't that much of a catch. But at least he was here to stay.

He considered the contents of his room. A small hunting

trophy, the glass-eyed head of a lynx, on the wall beside a poster of a tank crushing another tank adorned with a Hitler moustache – he dutifully collected anti-Nazi memorabilia but here on the steppe the war seemed very far way – his rifle, a red Young Pioneer scarf from his younger days, a book of Konstantin Simenov's poems . . . Yury himself often conceived luminous phrases but he could never utter them.

He heard a car draw up outside. A tractor was commonplace, a car an event. He peered through the lace curtains. A punished black Zil coated with dust. Two men were climbing out, an Army officer in a brown uniform and a civilian in a grey jacket and open-neck white shirt. Fear stirred inside Yury, although he couldn't imagine why.

His father called from the verandah: 'Yury, you've got visitors.' Yury could hear the apprehension in his voice. He changed into a dark blue shirt, slicked his hair with water and went outside.

They were sitting on the rickety chairs beside the wooden table drinking tea. The officer was a colonel; he had a bald head, startling eyebrows and a humorous mouth. The civilian had dishevelled features and pointed ears; he popped a cube of sugar into his mouth and sucked his tea through it. Alexander was walking towards the silver birch trees at the end of the vegetable garden.

The colonel said: 'I'm from Stalingrad, Comrade Pokrovsky is from Moscow. Have you ever been to Moscow, Yury?'

Yury shook his head. He wondered if Pokrovsky was NKVD.

'Or Stalingrad?'

'No, Comrade colonel.'

'Ah, you Siberians. You're very insular – if that's the right word for more than 4 million square miles of the Soviet Union. What's the farthest you've been from home?'

'I've been to Novosibirsk,' Yury told him.

'Novosibirsk! Forty miles from here. Well, I have news for you Yury. You're going farther afield. To Akhtubinsk, eighty miles east of Stalingrad. Please explain, Comrade

23

Pokrovsky.'

The civilian swallowed the dissolved sugar and said to Yury: 'You are going to serve your country. God knows, you might even become a Hero of the Soviet Union.'

Yury's father interrupted. 'He has a bad heart. I have the documents . . . ' The weathered lines on his face took on angles of worry.

'Heart condition? According to my information he has a heart murmur. A murmur, comrade! What is a murmur when Russia cries out in anguish?'

The colonel said to Yury's father: 'Of course I realise that farm work is just as important as military service,' and Pokrovsky said: 'Not that there seems to be much work going on round here. Haven't you heard about the war effort?'

'We've just finished harvesting one crop. Tomorrow we start on the wheat.' He spoke with dignity, pointing at the golden fields stroked by a breeze.

'You Siberians,' the colonel remarked. 'You don't stay on the defensive long, do you? Ask the Germans, you've taught them a lesson or two.'

Yury, his emotions competing – apprehension complicated by faint arousal of bravado – waited to find out what the two men wanted.

Pokrovsky spoke. 'Siberians? Very courageous.' He stroked one crumpled cheek. 'But don't forget the glorious example given by the Muscovites. And by Comrade Stalin. Did you read his speech on November 7th last year?' Pokrovsky looked quizzically at Yury.

Yury tried to remember some dashing phrase from the speech on the 24th anniversary of the Revolution. It had certainly been a stirring address.

Pokrovsky said: 'I was in Red Square when he spoke. What a setting. Troops massed in front of the Kremlin, German and Russian guns rumbling forty miles away and Stalin, The Boss, inspired.'

His voice was curiously flat for such an evocation. Then he began to quote. '"Comrades, Red Army and Red Navy men, officers and political workers, men and women partisans! The whole world is looking upon you as the power capable of destroying the German robber hordes! The enslaved peoples of Europe are looking upon you as their liberators . . . Be worthy of this great mission."'

Yury imagined the little man with the bushy moustache standing on Lenin's tomb. Heard his Georgian accents on a breeze stealing through the Urals.

"' . . . Death to the German Invaders. Long live our glorious country, its freedom and independence. Under the banner of Lenin – onward to victory."'

Without changing his tone, Pokrovsky said: 'Do you believe in those qualities, Yury? Freedom for instance?'

'Of course,' Yury replied, surprised.

'Of course, he's a Siberian,' said the colonel who was apparently obsessed with their matchless qualities.

Pokrovsky seemed satisfied. 'As you may have guessed it is your abilities as a hunter that interest us. I understand you're the best shot in the Novosibirsk *oblast*?'

'Second best,' Yury said promptly. 'My father is the champion.'

His father took off his black peaked cap and rotated it slowly on his lap.

'But a little too old to fight, eh?' The colonel smiled, offering commiseration.

As the sun reached inside the verandah through the fretted eaves steam rose from the dew-soaked floorboards. A tractor clattered lazily in the distance.

Pokrovsky said: 'There are ten of you. The best shots in the Soviet Union. You will all be reporting to Akhtubinsk. There will be a competition.'

He paused. He enjoyed effect. The colonel took over and Yury sensed that there was little harmony between the two of them. As he talked creases on his forehead pushed at the baldness above them.

'The other nine are Red Army. Marksmen. But you apparently are exceptional. Your prowess reached the ears of the military commander of the area and he told us about you.'

Yury's mother peered from the doorway. She was

25

smoothing her dress, printed with blue cornflowers, and her plump features were anxious.

Her husband waved her away. 'You will forgive me, comrades,' he said in a tone that didn't seek forgiveness, 'but would you please tell me what this is all about?'

Pokrovsky popped another lump of sugar into his mouth. He seemed to be debating with himself. Finally he said: 'As you know, the Germans attacked Stalingrad last month. The battle is still being fought fiercely and I have no doubt we shall win. But the Germans have introduced a new tactic . . .'

The colonel explained: 'The Germans are very good at propaganda. They know we are going to win the Battle of Stalingrad' – he didn't sound quite as convinced as Pokrovsky – 'and so they have to find a hero to bolster their faith. Well, they've found one. His name is Meister and he's a sniper. The best. Ten Russians killed, each with one bullet, in one week. Very soon the German people will be hearing about this young Aryan warrior with eyes like a hawk.' The colonel smiled. 'We have to beat the propagandists to the draw.'

Emotions not entirely unpleasant expanded inside Yury. 'But surely these other marksmen from the Red Army are better than me?'

'That,' Pokrovsky said, standing up, 'is what we are going to find out at Akhtubinsk. Come, pack your things, we haven't much time.'

Yury's father said: 'Do you have any authority, any papers?'

'Authority?' Pokrovsky spun out another pause. Then: 'Oh, we have authority all right. From the Kremlin. After all, the duel will be fought in the City of Stalin.'

***

A rat ran past Antonov, pausing at the mouth of the tunnel, a disused sewer, before jumping into the mud-grey waters of the Volga to swim to the east bank where there was still plenty of food. Antonov doubted whether it would make it: the Red Army had trouble enough getting across.

Where was Razin?

He shivered. The wet-cold of the tunnel had none of yesterday's expectancy about it. Antonov yearned for snow, but according to the locals – there were said to be 30,000 still on the west bank – it wouldn't settle until November.

These people professed to dread winter. Antonov suspected that, like Siberians, they deluded themselves. Summer was merely a ripening: winter was truth – the steppe, white and sweet, cold and lonely, animal tracks leading you into the muffled taiga, the song of cross-country skis on polished snow, blue-bright days with ice dust sparkling on the air, and in the evenings kerosene lamps and a glowing stove beckoning you home.

Antonov felt that when his parents had waved goodbye to him outside the cottage, Alexander beside them smiling tremulously, they should have been framed in falling snow. Instead the snapshot in his mind was glazed with late-summer heat. Just the same, whenever he studied the photograph, he felt as though a dressing had just been removed from a wound.

He heard a disturbance at the other end of the tunnel that had been fractured by a shell. He reached for his rifle. 'Razin?'

No reply. He aimed his rifle into the darkness and a young voice said: 'Don't shoot,' although there wasn't any fear in it.

The boy reached the light from the river exit and offered Antonov a bucket. 'Thirsty? It's been boiled.' One of the water boys who quenched the Russian soldiers' thirst and fed them scraps of food. They also fraternised with the Germans, subsequently describing uniforms and positions to the commanders of the encircled 62nd Army.

'No thanks.' Antonov grinned at him; his face was sharp and starved; Antonov had read Dickens at school and he reminded him of a pickpocket in *Oliver Twist*. 'What's your name?'

'Misha.'

'Shouldn't you be on the other side of the river, Misha?'

Although he was only eighteen Antonov felt paternal. He

27

had discovered that war confused age.

'No point. I can only help over here. In any case the kids on the other side have got families.'

'You haven't?'

'My parents were killed on the thirteenth.'

The thirteenth of September, a Sunday, was the day when the Germans had launched an all-out assault on the city. One month ago and the boy spoke as though he had lost his parents when he was in the cradle. War also confused time.

'I'm sorry,' Antonov said.

Misha said: 'My father was a baker. He used to bake bread for the militia. What was your father?'

'He's still alive,' Antonov said. 'He works on a State farm. We grow a lot of grain. Maybe some of it found its way into your father's bread.'

Misha shook his head. 'Our flour came from the steppe near here. But the Fritzes flattened all the corn. Soon we'll flatten theirs. Won't we?' he asked.

'Of course. How old are you, Misha?'

The boy said he was nine and then, as though ashamed of the admission, picked up his bucket and crawled back along the tunnel.

Where was Razin?

* * *

Before departing for the Red Army transit camp Antonov had been allowed to see Tasya.

'In the bad old days of serfdom,' the colonel told him in the back of the Zil, 'it was a punishment to be drafted. But you were allowed seven days in which to drink and fornicate before you left. Today you've got time for a kiss.'

'But today it's an honour to serve in the army,' Pokrovsky reminded both of them. 'Life in the barracks is as good as anywhere else. And life is good everywhere in the Soviet Union,' he reminded himself. 'You have a good education, good food, fair wages, paid holidays . . .' Pokrovsky had a tendency to recite.

28

Yury who had never doubted any of this nodded as he watched his home recede in the distance. A lone horseman stood on the brow of a sloping wheatfield.

Tasya was wearing a white blouse embroidered in silk with red and blue daisies. Her flaxen hair was polished and thickly coiled and he realised she had been expecting him. The driver of the Zil, it materialised, was also a photographer and it just happened that he had a camera and plates with him.

Yury kissed Tasya, feeling her lips part slightly. But the farewell wasn't complicated by any of the carnal visions that had visited him that morning.

Twenty-four hours later he was in the Red Army. Bewildered by the casual and coarse attitudes of his new comrades, shocked by instant antagonisms, discovering what he had always known but never appreciated, that the Soviet Union consists of many races.

Of the other nine marksmen assembled at Akhtubinsk one was a lieutenant, evacuated from beleaguered Leningrad and billeted in a separate hut, one was a scheming Georgian, four were Muscovites and full of it, two were Ukrainians and one was an Uzbek from Samarkand who looked like a Bedouin.

On the first day Antonov, the only new recruit in the group, was given an ill-fitting uniform, a Mosin-Nagant, mess tin and irons, two grey blankets and a mattress filled with straw. The food was uneatable but by the second day he was wolfing it down.

On that day the ten competitors went to the range. In the truck taking them there the Muscovites kept themselves to themselves but talked about Antonov.

'I hear he uses barleycorn for sights.'

'Shoots with a flintlock.'

'Good at shooting bears – if they're big enough.'

As Antonov's rivals had been in the Army for some time they were familiar with the heavy Mosin-Nagants whereas he had only used a light hunting rifle.

He and the lieutenant scored the least points.

On the third day he had his hair cropped and his wallet stolen from his tunic while he was shaving in the communal

29

wash-house. The wallet was returned later; nothing was missing, but a photograph of Tasya, taken on the day of his departure, had been embellished with pudenda and balloon breasts. A scrawled caption compared her to a cow about to fornicate with a yokel.

Antonov sat quietly on the edge of his bed for a while, unable to comprehend such grossness. They were all Soviets so why should there be such hostility to someone from the steppe? However that sort of antagonism narrowed the field; the perpetrator had to be from a city. He glanced at the four Muscovites who had formed an enclave at one end of the billet; two looked faintly embarrassed, one was smiling, the fourth, grey-faced and built like a wrestler, lay on his back, hands behind his head, scrutinising the corrugated-iron ceiling.

Antonov who had never experienced physical violence walked over to his bed and showed him the photograph. 'Did you do this?'

Yawning, the Muscovite commented obcenely on the photograph.

Antonov pulled him up by his tunic and drew back his fist to hit him but suddenly he wasn't there and then *he* was attacking with fists, and booted feet. Antonov fell against the wall, hands in front of his face to protect himself from the fusillade of blows.

'Of course we have Don Cossack blood in our veins,' his father said as, guns in their hands, they waited for movement in the snow-quiet taiga.

And now his fist was a rifle and he was peering through the sights, lowering the barrel, deviating to allow for evasive tactics. And now the fist was a bullet, on target. The Muscovite staggered back, hit the far wall and slid bloodily to the floor.

After that no one commented upon Antonov's rustic background.

'I hear,' Pokrovsky said later, 'that you've been brawling.'

Antonov, standing to attention in front of Pokrovsky's desk in a small hut that smelled of carbolic, didn't reply: his split lip

30

and swollen cheeks answered the question.

'We should think ourselves lucky he didn't damage your eyes.'

We?

'I'm out of the competition,' Antonov said.

Pokrovsky touched one pointed ear, ran his fingers down his lined cheek. 'I have arranged for you to be given one more chance,' he said. 'The day after tomorrow. Just nine of you. The lieutenant has departed.' He paused. 'But don't be misled by regional differences. We have more than fifty languages in the Soviet Union but we speak with one tongue.' He slipped an oblong of sugar into his mouth and drank some tea. 'Now to business.'

He told Antonov that he had one day in which to make an ally of his Mosin-Nagant. He pointed at an ammunition box containing yellow-tipped 7.62 mm ammunition. 'Yours. There's a forest five kilometres from here. Not unlike the taiga near your home.' Pokrovsky almost smiled.

Sitting in the Zil beside Pokrovsky who was driving, Antonov decided that he had glimpsed an unsuspected truth. That kindness is not necessarily selfless. But none the worse for that, he supposed.

The forest, cathedral vaults of pine and congregations of silver birch, *was* similar to the taiga and he shot all day, taking one break, eating black bread smeared with caviar and drinking Narzan mineral water while Pokrovsky drank beer, until the gun was part of him and the yellow-tipped bullets were punching out the hearts of the black and white targets, buckling the cans that Pokrovsky threw into the air.

On the following day he and the Muscovite with whom he had fought finished ahead of the other competitors. It had to be him, of course. When the two of them shot it out Antonov won by one point.

Afterwards the Muscovite shook his hand and Antonov learned another truth although he wasn't sure what it was.

***

31

When Razin returned to the tunnel he told Antonov that a Russian sniper had been shot between the eyes in a church near Ninth of January Square. 'Meister must have been on his way to Mamaev Hill,' Razin said.

'The obvious place.'

'So we'll stay put here for a while.' Razin squatted next to Antonov. 'And another thing – the Fritzes are launching an all-out attack on the north of the city tomorrow.'

CHAPTER FIVE

October 14. The sun, it was rumoured, was shining but beneath the acrid grime of the German assault there was little hope of confirming this.

Meister watched the attack from a ruined toy factory, but it was difficult to grasp what was happening because the senses, stunned by the bombardment, lied.

It was just before midday. According to information obtained by Lanz, five divisions, three infantry and two panzer, were attacking on a front three miles wide. Their objective: to dislodge the Russians from their last footholds in the industrial north and claim the city.

It was, asserted Lanz, the final assault; but his tone questioned his words.

Meister picked up a toy rifle with a sparkling red star on its butt. He aimed it at a doll with eggshell-blue eyes and fuzzy blonde hair sitting on a shelf; but he didn't pull the trigger because the doll suddenly became his sister. He lowered the rifle; his head was full of noise.

Lanz drew a diagram in the dust on the floor – the main factories, Red October, Barricade and Tractor Plant, lying between railroad and river. 'They say that if we capture these we've won. And do you know what they are?'

Meister shrugged.

'Heaps of bricks. That's what we're fighting for, bricks.'

Another wave of aircraft flew overhead to add their bombs

to the shells and mortars falling on the Russians. Occasionally Yaks and Migs got among the bombers.

The tormented ground continued to tremble. The doll fell from the shelf and lay on its side in the dust.

***

To an extent Meister attributed his presence in Stalingrad to his sister, Magdalena, who was two years older than him. When, reluctantly, she had taken him as an adolescent to a café in Hamburg protruding over the water of the Binnenalster he had observed that she paid most attention, albeit not transparently, to the young men who had the most to offer – a future, perhaps, in the SS or Luftwaffe combined with athletic prowess, looks and wealth and some indefinable attraction that he merely sensed.

Knowing that he possessed none of the obvious assets – an aptitude for languages was hardly an entrée – suspecting that he lacked the more subtle accomplishments, Meister had set about rectifying this state of affairs. Thus he had become not only a sharp-shooter on the rifle range but a very smart young man indeed with occasional access to his father's Mercedes-Benz and a reputation as a wit that, when the natural flow ran dry, had to be augmented by memorised aphorisms from a book of quotations.

The reputation and, in fact, the whole charade was soon demolished by Elzbeth. 'That sounds suspiciously like Samuel Johnson,' she said one day as, with elaborate nonchalance, he entertained her in one of the lounges of the Vier Jahreszeiten. 'So he thought of it as well,' Meister blustered; but his cheeks felt as though they were steaming.

'Why do you bother, Karl? Be yourself.'

What confused him was that as Elzbeth was one of Magdalena's acquaintances, one of the set, she should accept his epigrams, borrowed or otherwise, without question. Her blonde hair made small and deceptively innocent wings in front of her ears.

'How do we know our true selves? We're all guided,

34

influenced.'

'Then we should resist,' she said, 'before it's too late.'

And so, abandoning affectation, he took her boating on the Aussenalster and walking in the countryside, and one Sunday morning he escorted her to the fish market at St. Pauli where at a stall thronged with young people who didn't belong to the set they breakfasted on würst thickly daubed with mustard. And later that day he kissed her in the back of the Mercedes-Benz on a wharf overlooking the Elbe.

He joined the army two days after he was pictured with Elzbeth in the German newspapers receiving the cup for marksmanship in Berlin. He was trained as a sniper and two months later he was in Stalingrad.

***

'I presume,' Lanz said, raising his voice to compete with the bombardment, 'you were one of the Young Folk.'

'Of course. And Hitler Youth.'

He had been given a dagger engraved with the words BLOOD AND HONOUR and told that he could now defend his brown-shirt and uniform with it. At college grace had always been recited before meals; it had asserted that God had sent Hitler to save Germany.

'Did you belong to any organisation?' Meister asked.

'The Young Offenders' Association.' Lanz was drinking vodka from an Army-issue flask and he was a little drunk; a lot of the troops were. 'Did you believe all that Nazi shit they taught you?' Lanz asked.

'I believed what I saw. A new deal for Germany. A sense of purpose. Equality.'

'Unless you happened to be a Jew.'

Meister didn't reply. He had been uneasy about the Jewish problem since the night in November, 1938, when he had seen a mob pillage a synagogue in Hamburg. His father, holding his hand on the sidewalk, had laughed as uproariously at the distraught rabbi as he had at the clowns at the circus a few days earlier.

35

A Katyusha exploded nearby, its bellow distinct from the other explosions.

Lanz said: 'And do you believe in all this?' gesturing towards the gunfire.

'I believe the Bolsheviks have got to be defeated.'

'Bolsheviks! Don't you realise that the end product of National Socialism and Communism is the same?'

It had never occurred to Meister. He searched his aching mind for a devastating retort. Finally he said: 'National Socialism is the equal distribution of benefits: Communism is the equal distribution of poverty.'

He thought that was neat; he doubted whether Elzbeth would have agreed.

Lanz rubbed at his bald patch as though he were trying to remove it. It looked like a Jewish skull-cap, Meister thought.

Lanz swigged vodka. 'And I suppose you think we're going to beat the Bolsheviks?'

'We've captured great tracts of Russia.'

'Ah, but Russia goes on forever. Want a drink?' offering the flask to Meister.

'You know I don't drink.'

'Christ! What *do* you do except spout propaganda? What did I do to deserve this, nursemaid to a college kid? Have you ever had a woman?' he asked abruptly.

'Of course,' Meister lied.

'One like this?' Lanz took a creased photograph of a naked woman wearing stiletto-heeled shoes from his wallet and showed it to Meister. She was smoking a cigarette in a holder and smiling coyly at the camera.

'Prettier than that,' Meister told Lanz

'So who's looking at her face?'

Remembering the quivering embraces with Elzbeth in the back of the Mercedes-Benz, the tentative, exploratory caresses, Meister was ashamed of the flicker of arousal he had experienced when he had looked at the photograph.

Lanz said: 'Have you got a photograph of your girl?'

'No,' Meister said, but his hand strayed to the pocket of his tunic where, beneath studio lights, Elzbeth lay close to his heart.

Lanz shrugged. 'Did you expect it to be like this?' he asked, waving the flask towards the battle in the north of the city.

'I don't think anyone realised how tough the Russians are.'

'If you'd been at Moscow you would have got the general idea.'

'I suppose I imagined killing and suffering. But not massacre – on both sides.'

'Can you give me one good reason why I should look after you?' Lanz asked.

'None.'

'Well, I can. Being with you I stand a better chance of surviving. And surviving is what I'm good at. So don't ever think I'm doing it for you.'

'I never thought that,' Meister said.

'It was your sort of people that got us into this. Prussians, Junkers.'

'The French got us into this,' said Meister, resurrecting the lectures at college. 'And the British. The Treaty of Versailles that bled us white.'

'What I meant,' Lanz said, choosing his words with drunken care, 'was that it was your sort got us into the first war. If that hadn't happened there wouldn't have been a Treaty of Versailles. And maybe we would never have heard of this arschloch of a place.'

But the last war was too long ago for argument.

'Were you a successful thief?' Meister asked.

'Watch your wallet,' Lanz said.

'They say the Russians have got a division of criminals in the 62nd Army.'

'The 112th. Beware of them. They won't get any medals but they'll survive. Like me.' Lanz picked up a toy soldier and pocketed it. 'For my son,' he said.

'I didn't know you were married.'

'I'm not.' Lanz slipped another soldier into his pocket. 'They tell me Antonov has got a nanny too. An old soldier from the Ukraine. Old soldiers, they're survivors too.'

Meister picked up his field-glasses and peered through a

shell-hole in the wall. He saw a woman in black pushing a pram filled with rubble; she was obviously crazy but, Meister wondered, had she been sane before the battle began? He saw a Persian cat picking its way around a crater and the rotting corpse of a Russian soldier smiling at him from beneath a cloud of flies.

He focussed the field-glasses on the fighting. A ragged line of German soldiers was advancing into the smoke. A young officer was urging them forward.

And for a moment it seemed to him that the officer and his men were probing the cordite mists for some truth to which they hadn't yet been introduced.

The Katyusha that exploded in their midst must have killed them all.

Then a breeze crossed the Volga breaching gaps in the smoke and through one of them Meister saw Antonov.

CHAPTER SIX

Antonov, searching for Meister in the vacuum behind the German attack, felt naked as the smoke parted around him.

He looked to his left. A factory of sorts built on a rise, long and squat, roofless and windowless, walls pocked by shells and bullets. Good cover, good vantage . . .

He threw himself to the ground taking Razin with him. The bullet hit the street lamp at the level where their heads had been. Glancing up, Antonov saw the bright wound in the green-painted metal.

The last thing he noticed before smoke swathed them again was a woman pushing a pram, searching, it occurred to him, for the past.

Back in the tunnel Razin's rat was waiting for them. Its name was Boris and Razin maintained that it was shell-shocked; it had wandered into the tunnel but, unlike its fellows, had shown no inclination to swim the Volga; instead it had circled the two of them, sitting down from time to time to favour them with a pink-eyed stare. It had impudent whiskers and protruding teeth and at times Antonov felt that Razin was more concerned about its welfare than the outcome of the vendetta with Meister.

Throwing Boris crumbs of black bread, Razin said: 'A much maligned beast, Comrade Rat. Why? Because he's small and quick and he gets hungry. Now if he were an elephant he would be venerated. And yet one elephant can do more damage in five minutes than a rat can do in a lifetime.'

Antonov said: 'Elephants provide ivory; rats spread the plague.'

'Not Boris.' Razin threw him a morsel of cheese. 'Story-tellers through the ages have a lot to answer for. If an animal isn't physically attractive then it's the villain. What sort of philosophy is that to teach the young? Small wonder the school bully beats up the poor little bastard with buck teeth and muscles in the wrong places.'

The rat's whiskers moved busily as it ate the cheese.

'What about poor old Reynard?' Razin warmed to his theme. 'Just because he's got a long nose and likes chicken for dinner he's the devil incarnate. But everyone is supposed to love pussy cats. And what do they do? They catch birds and tease them till they die.'

'Foxes steal,' Antonov said.

'Steal?' Razin, pulling at his drooping moustache, looked incredulously at Antonov. 'Do you think Reynard knows the meaning of *steal*? He just spots a good meal and gets it the best way he can. He's clever: the story-tellers have made him cunning.'

The tunnel shook as a shell exploded near by. A brick fell from the curved roof but the rat nibbled on.

Razin extended an eloquent, battle-dirty hand. 'And what will the tellers of tales make of all this?' long fingers clasping Stalingrad in the palm of his hand. 'Glory, that's what. Heroism. Knights in shining armour. And not just the story-tellers, the writers of school history books too. Because, you see, that's where all this begins,' holding his hand aloft. 'In the schoolroom. Did you ever read about the misery of war in the classroom?'

Antonov cast his mind back to the rows of desks with their pencilled grooves, inkwells filled with purple ink made from powder and water; heard the scratch of chalk on blackboard, smelled disinfectant and modelling-clay and pencil sharpen-ings. He shook his head. No, war had always been glorious, especially the Civil War.

'Small wonder we grow up the way we do. The next

40

revolution should be in the schoolroom.'

Faintly they heard German voices chanting: 'Russians, you'll soon be blowing bubbles in the Volga.'

'But surely,' Antonov protested, 'war brings out the best in people. Bravery, sacrifice . . . ' Antonov tried to free the words that were always imprisoned inside him.

'Try survival,' Razin said. He laid his head on a red cushion he had removed from a wrecked house. 'Isn't that why we're cowering in a sewer with Boris?'

Antonov rested his back against the wall of the tunnel. The tunnel was a telescope and through one end he saw a wooden balcony float past on the river with an old man clinging to the balustrade.

He said: 'I can't understand why you're here at all. You know, with the prospects you had.'

'What do you want from me? Unhappy childhood? Young life permanently scarred? Son of a great man unable to emulate his father?'

Antonov who wanted none of these things began to clean his rifle.

'I had a happy childhood,' Razin told him. 'I collected stamps,' as though that summed it up and in a way it did. 'We lived in a neat little house in Kiev, in Lipki, with a white fence round it and when I close my eyes I can hear the breeze in the lime trees and feel the stickiness on the leaves and smell the river, the Dnieper, and hear the bells on the trams and, do you know, it's more real than this. They say that when you grow old the past is more real than the present so maybe I've got older quicker than most. Old soldiers do, I suppose.'

Razin's voice aged.

'And I remember the poplars – lots of trees in my memories – and the chestnuts candlelit in spring and the wide skies, and window-shopping with my parents although there wasn't much in the windows but it didn't matter – that's where people make mistakes about upbringing, deprivation doesn't mean a damn thing – and funnily enough the breathy smell from the metro station, Mayakovskaya. Have you heard the proverb, "If you use your tongue you'll get to Kiev"?'

When Antonov said he hadn't Razin said: 'To be honest I never knew what it meant. But when Russians are stumped for an explanation for anything they make up a proverb. Proverbs and superstitions, the clues to our souls.'

Antonov wiped a drop of oil from the trigger of the rifle. He pressed the butt into his shoulder and the rifle became part of him.

'And the cinema,' Razin remembered, reaching for the vodka. 'Tarzan and Tom Mix and Charlie Chaplin and, every other week, the *Battleship Potemkin*. And the smell of the cinema, the Shantser – celluloid and cheap scent and cigarette smoke. Smells, how would memories live without them? *And* the taste of lipstick.' Razin smiled, showing yellow teeth.

Silence except for the muted noise of battle. Was that all? 'I still don't understand,' Antonov said tentatively.

'Because there's nothing to understand. You think there has to be a reason for everything. Wrong. Things just happen. Sorry to disappoint you.' Razin swigged vodka. 'But if you must have a reason perhaps it was happiness. I was too happy.'

Not good enough, Antonov thought.

'Content, perhaps. And secure. Yes, despite the Revolution and the Civil War, I was secure. I didn't question anything. I was complacent. Do you know something, Yury? That's what Communism teaches you, complacency. If you're not very careful you accept everything it has to offer you, a recitation of values.'

'But you rebelled?'

'Not in the conventional sense. No speeches, no banners, no handcuffs chaining me to railings. I was studying law at the university in Kiev, reciting it, and one day I just got up from my desk, walked out of class and joined the army.'

'It could be argued that you were shirking responsibility.'

'Watch it, comrade, you're beginning to sound like a commissar.'

Yury worked the bolt of his rifle; it made comforting, oil-snug noises. 'If you feel like that about Communism you shouldn't be fighting for it.'

'Who's fighting for Communism? Every soldier I've met is fighting for Russia. In any case I'm not fighting, am I? I'm nursing.'

'You fought for Moscow.'

'Survival, comrade. And I was shit-scared at Moscow.'

'Perhaps you have to be scared to be brave?'

'Leave the philosophising to me,' Razin said.

Philosophising? Nothing that Razin said seemed to have any pattern. But that was the case with any of the philosophers – admittedly few – that Yury had read: they only complicated logic.

In the confusing light from the river the lines on Razin's face, cheek to jaw, looked deeper than usual, exaggerated, probably, by the bristles his cut-throat razor had missed while he shaved with cold water and carbolic soap during a bombardment. Razin, the old soldier, kept himself neat.

He also worried about his health. He suffered from boils and mysterious internal pains but, all things considered, he looked astonishingly healthy.

Recalling the conversation with one of the soldiers who had jumped into the crater, Antonov asked him about the Ukrainians. Had some of them joined the Germans? Was such treachery possible in the Soviet Union?

'You wouldn't understand. Your kitbag's still full of school books. Who am I to disillusion you?'

An oil-slick swimming with rainbow patterns slid past the tunnel on the muddy water. Boris, belly against the brickwork floor, sat like a dog.

Razin asked: 'Which is most important to you, the Soviet Union or your republic?'

'My country and then my republic of course,' said Antonov who had never thought about it before.

'Ah, but I forgot, your republic *is* Russia. Stupid of me. But some day . . . ' With one finger he felt the fur inside a crease on his cheek.

'You didn't answer *my* question about the Ukrainians.'

'Didn't I? You probably won't believe this but a lot of Ukrainians were praying that the Germans would annihilate

43

the Russians. And why not? The west of the Ukraine was part of Poland until Stalin grabbed it in 1939. And the feeling in the east wasn't much different. You see the idiot Ukrainians think they have an identity. So what did the Boss do? Stamped upon it, purged it, stole the harvest so that people starved . . . Do you wonder that some of them opened their arms to the Fritzes. And occasionally their legs? And why?'

Antonov wished he would stop asking questions.

'Because the Germans promised to let them have their own government, that's why.'

'Did they get it?'

'They got it all right. For five days. Then the Germans broke it up. Locked up all the hot shots. Killed the Jews and anyone who got in their way. You see the Germans want *lebensraum*, living space, and what better place than the Ukraine?'

'And that's the only reason the Ukrainians are fighting the Germans now?'

'Not the only reason. Mother Russia has a broad embrace.'

Antonov said: 'One last thing. Why didn't we know that Germany was going to attack?'

'Do you remember the days not so long ago when Hitler and the Boss were like this?' Razin entwined two fingers. 'Well, they were both buying time, trying to fool each other. But Stalin needed more time . . .'

'I think,' Antonov said, 'that I'd better throw those school books out of my kit-bag.'

He looked at Boris but the rat was asleep.

***

Misha arrived half an hour later bringing boiled water, warm bread and *makhorka*. Razin took some of the coarse black tobacco and rolled himself a cigarette with a strip of *Red Star*.

'So,' Razin said, 'how's the battle going?'

'We're fighting for every inch of ground,' Misha quoted. Losing, thought Antonov, flexing his new awareness. 'Zholudev's guards are fantastic. They're tall and very

44

straight and they wear paratroop uniforms and they fight with daggers and bayonets.'

'The best,' Razin agreed.

'I saw them go into a cellar and kill all the Fritzes inside. One of them threw a body over his shoulder on his bayonet as though it were a sandbag.'

Misha's eyes were dark and bright in his pale face; the skin on his cheekbones had a transparent quality about it and his knees below his short trousers were like little fists; but he was full of importance.

'Where are they fighting now?' Razin asked.

'In the Tractor Plant Stadium.'

'Shit,' Razin said.

'When the Guards die they shout: "For country and Stalin! We shall never surrender!"'

'And do you know what units are fighting there?'

'Oh yes, I know.'

'But you're not going to tell us?'

'Why do you want to know?' Misha asked.

'We're supposed to be on the same side,' Razin said.

'Can I have a cigarette? A real cigarette.'

Razin gave him a *papirosy*.

Misha lit the cardboard-tube cigarette and drew on it inhaling deeply; like most Russians he made a meal of a smoke.

'Don't you trust us?' Antonov asked.

'I was told not to tell anyone about the German units until I got to headquarters.'

'Then you must do what you're told.'

'I suppose you're different,' Misha said. 'The 94th and the 389th Infantry. Fourteenth and 24th Panzers and the 100th Jäger.'

'And Meister?'

'That's why I came here. He's in the toy factory.'

Remembering the lessons about war he had learned at school in Hamburg? Antonov wondered what Hamburg was like. Not much different, perhaps, from Novosibirsk. Or Stalingrad as it had once been.

45

He took out his wallet and extracted a photograph of Meister taken from the German forces magazine *Signal*. He looked very sleek and sophisticated standing beside a poised blonde, smiling over his trophy; but the smile was borrowed and it didn't fit his face. In that moment Antonov the hunter glimpsed uncertainty in his prey.

'How did you get warm bread?' Razin asked Misha.

'It's old bread heated on a primus. I like the smell of warm bread. It makes me think of early mornings before the Germans came.'

'Did you help in the bakery?' Antonov asked.

'During the school holidays. With the cakes. Sometimes I make a small one for myself. We made lots of cakes on national days. My father said national days were a baker's icing-sugar.'

Antonov knew what he meant. Stick a pin in a calendar and you stood a good change of spearing a national day. New Year, Lenin's death, May Day, Young Pioneers, Komsomol, the Revolution . . . In his patch of Siberia the bakers made rings of pastry symbolising the sun for *Maslennitsa*, the end of winter.

'Papa made lots of jokes,' Misha said. 'He used to make biscuits with currants in them and he called them fly-biscuits. He was small and neat and his hands were always very clean when they weren't covered in flour. When he dipped his hands in flour he looked as if he was wearing white gloves.'

'Did your mother work in the bakery, too?'

'Sometimes, if there was a rush. A lot of people getting married in the Palace of Weddings perhaps. She was taller than Papa and she used to tell him not to be silly when he made his jokes but often when she turned her head I saw her laughing. She used to help me with my homework. She said she wanted me to become a doctor. I didn't want to become one: I wanted to be a soldier.'

'No brothers or sisters?'

'I had a brother once but I never saw him. My mother went to hospital with him inside her but she came back without him. She said it was God's will but after that she never talked

46

about it. I remember the first day Papa came back from hospital. He went to the bakery and threw away a cake he had baked. It had a little silver cradle on it. The bomb fell on the bakery when my mother was taking my father his breakfast,' Misha said. 'Eggs and cold sausage – he couldn't stand bread.'

He turned his face away from them puffing furiously on his cigarette. After a few moments he said: 'You could get Meister now. From behind the factory.'

Antonov didn't know how to explain but it wasn't right to shoot Meister in the back and he knew that was stupid, a target was a target.

Misha said to Antonov: 'Shouldn't you be out there looking for him?'

'We have been,' Antonov said.

'Yury nearly got his head blown off,' Razin said.

'You mean the *svoloch* missed?' Misha's sharp features registered disbelief.

'Don't swear,' Antonov admonished him. 'No, he didn't exactly miss: I anticipated him.'

'Anticipated?' Misha thought about it. 'You mean you ducked?'

'Anticipated first. There's no point in ducking when someone's shooting at you. It's always too late. But when you hear the crack then you know you're okay because the crack is caused by the vacuum behind the bullet.'

Misha wasn't interested in vacuums. 'He *is* good, isn't he?' and Antonov realised that as far as the boy was concerned it had to be a battle between aces. As far as the Red Army was concerned, come to that. And the Soviet people.

'The best,' Antonov said.

'No, you're the best. You'll get him.'

'With your help.' Antonov smiled at him.

'Then why don't you go after him now? He won't be expecting you.'

'Want to bet?'

Misha shrugged. You know best, the shrug said, but I think you're wrong. Nipping out his cigarette, dropping the butt in the top pocket of the grey jacket that he had outgrown, gathering his importance around him like a cloak, Misha disappeared down the tunnel.

'I suppose he's right,' Antonov said. 'We'd better go and get him before he finds us.'

'He won't find us here.'

'We can't spend the rest of our lives in a sewer.'

'How long will our lives last out there?'

'Longer than they would at the Red October or Barricade factories.'

'True.' Razin stood up and stretched. 'Come on, follow nanny.'

***

Two days later Antonov was summoned to 62nd Army headquarters. The sergeant who found him in the tunnel said: 'Misha told us you were here,' a flake of disapproval in his voice.

General Vasili Ivanovich Chuikov, forty-two, was waiting for him in his bunker in one of the ravines on the west bank.

He was a chunky man with a soft bush of black hair, a boxer's face and a mouthful of gold teeth. His skin had erupted in sores caused by nervous strain. Not only was he responsible for the besieged army, he had been besieged himself – by fire. German bombs had hit a cluster of oil tanks and burning fuel had swept through the dugouts on its way to the river; the torrent of flames continued for three days but Chuikov and his officers stayed put. When the Germans poured shells into the HQ they moved 500 yards to the north.

The troops respected him: he was one of them, a *frontovnik*, a front-liner, and a peasant, and when he first arrived he kicked the asses of the officers who fought campaigns far from the sound of battle. Rumour had it that there was no love lost between Chuikov, commander of the 62nd Army, and General Andrei Yeremenko, overall commander of the Stalingrad Front.

Two officers sat on either side of Chuikov. One was Antonov Krylov, chief of staff, the other, squat with a head made for butting, exuded aggression, but not even Razin, chronicler of gossip and rumours, knew who he was. Their faces were lit and hollowed by a kerosene lamp.

The chief of staff dismissed Razin and the officers lit cigarettes, Kazbecks. The cement bunker reeked of smoke. Antonov coughed; Chuikov offered him the packet; Antonov shook his head. 'No thank you, Comrade General.'

'So you don't smoke. Or drink?' Chuikov's voice was as hard as winter, but frayed with fatigue. And when Antonov shook his head: 'What do you do?'

'Kill Germans, Comrade General.' Antonov was startled by his words: they had a ring of impudence that he didn't feel; nerves, he supposed.

'We all do that, in our different ways.'

A radio operator handed Chuikov a message. Chuikov read it aloud. 'Surrounded. Have a little ammunition. Will fight to the last bullet.' Chuikov said: 'He always had a flair for the dramatic,' but he didn't say who the message was from.

He clasped bandaged hands and stared at Antonov. 'You know the situation in the north is desperate? The Germans have taken the Tractor Plant and our forces have been cut to ribbons. The 208th, the 193rd, the 37th, they're just numbers now. But God how they fought.'

The third officer looked from Chuikov to Antonov. He was on the small side but he looked as tough as a ram; and yet laughter had creased the corners of his eyes.

'Have you ever been in the thick of a battle?' Chuikov asked Antonov.

'No, Comrade General.'

'After a while death and suffering don't have much impact. Not when your belly is empty and your skull is full of noise. Your senses, you see, are bewildered. You smell mud and cordite and you see it and taste it and feel it. And the man next to you who has just had his jaw blown off seems as normal as a companion on an assembly line. Why, you even welcome the thrust of a bayonet. And death,' the general said.

'Come, come, Vassili,' the tough-looking officer said. 'This young man doesn't want to hear that sort of thing. Save it for your memoirs.'

'This,' Chuikov said to Antonov, 'is Comrade Nikita Khrushchev of the War Council of the Front. He is going to take you across the river.'

Bewildered, Antonov stared at Stalin's political emissary. Why did he have to cross the Volga with him? How could he shoot Meister over there?

But Chuikov wasn't to be diverted from the point he had been pursuing. 'I understand the sergeant found you hiding in a sewer.'

So that was it, Chuikov had no time for prima donnas who didn't share the suffering of his men.

'With respect, Comrade General,' Antonov protested, 'I only take shelter when Meister is looking for me.' Wrong, that sounded as though he ran away every time Meister picked up his rifle. 'You see,' he explained, 'there comes a time when I'm stalking Meister when he becomes aware of me. Then our roles become reversed. Then I have to go to ground. It's the same with him, when he comes looking for me and when I see him, I feel his presence then he takes cover.'

'In a sewer?'

'I don't know where he's hiding Comrade General.' Meister had left the toy factory.

'Then isn't it about time you found out? The Soviet people are waiting to hear about your glorious exploit. Killing one German! But first,' his tone wearily disgusted, 'Comrade Khrushchev wants to take you on a riverboat.'

Khrushchev said genially: 'We shan't be long. One day at the most. I think you will enjoy yourself.' The skin at the corners of his eyes crinkled with merriment.

'May I ask –'

'No you may not,' Khrushchev said. A Stuka, Jericho siren on its undercarriage screaming, swooped overhead; no one took any notice. 'I just wish,' Khrushchev said, 'that I were in your shoes.'

***

50

Tasya was waiting for him in a wooden cottage on the east bank near a white church with a green dome.

Her flaxen hair was braided and her lipstick glistened more brightly than he remembered and her figure seemed more defined.

'Hallo, Yury,' she said. She held out her hands. They had seen a film once in which the star, wearing a silk gown, lights shining on her hair, had made the same gesture to her lover returning from a foreign land.

'Hallo.' He held her hands and smiled, then frowned as flash bulbs exploded.

'Now kiss her,' said a cameraman.

And she was warm in his arms and her perfume smelled different, more expensive, and her lips were against his.

'Just once more,' said another photographer.

'Hey, come on,' said a middle-aged man with bunchy hair to the cameraman. 'Don't forget you only illustrate the stories we write.'

'Don't forget,' said the photographer, 'that you only write the captions for the pictures we take.'

They kissed again.

'What are you doing here?' Antonov asked.

'I came to see you.'

'What was that?' the reporter asked.

'I came to see him.'

Antonov looked around. The room, homely with rocking chairs, rush mats, a table with an embroidered runner on it, a stove and Lenin and Stalin on the walls, reminded him of the living room in Siberia; it even smelled of the same polish his mother used. It was a movie set and he and Tasya were the stars. He wished he was back on the other side of the Volga which was strange because the troops there were always wishing they were on the east bank because that was where the war ended.

The reporter said to Antonov: 'It must have been dangerous crossing the river to see your girl.'

Other journalists waited expectantly, pencils poised. 'Dangerous? Everyone would give a year's pay to get away

51

from the west bank.'

A voice in the background said: 'I'm sure I don't have to remind you that Yury is exhausted; that some of what he says shouldn't be quoted.'

The reporter with the bunchy hair said: 'When are you going to get Meister?'

'Soon.'

'How soon?'

'When I'm ready,' and someone said: '"When I'm ready," that's great.'

The reporter with the bunchy hair asked Tasya: 'What does it feel like to be engaged to a future Hero of the Soviet Union?'

Engaged?

Tasya squeezed his hand. 'It doesn't matter whether he's a hero or not,' she said. 'I always hoped that one day Yury and me . . .'

Antonov looked back through the weeks and saw a youth, a stranger, kissing Tasya after a Komsomol meeting and the stranger was himself.

'Did you hope that Comrade Antonov?'

'I hoped many things.'

'When you've killed Meister do you intend to get married immediately?'

'He hasn't asked me yet,' Tasya said coyly.

'But I thought – '

'We had an understanding.'

'So?' The reporter looked at Antonov.

'I've got to kill Meister first,' Antonov said.

'Of course.' A severely dressed woman journalist with a bosom like a bookshelf smiled understandingly. 'Are you close to Meister? Do you think the same way?'

'You would have to get a second opinion – from him.' Remarkable how he was beginning to use words.

'I was asking how *you* felt.'

'We're both snipers. We're both trying to kill each other. We must have something in common.'

'That wasn't what I was asking you,' the woman said, 'and

52

you know it,' but she didn't pursue it.

'What special qualities does a sniper have?' another journalist asked and Antonov told him because that was nearly always the first question anyone asked him. His replies were a recitation.

On the other side of the river he heard a German Ishak mortar, explosions like the neighing of a horse.

A plump reporter from *Izvestia* asked: 'Do you have a message for the Soviet people?'

The room was filling with smoke. Antonov could never understand why anyone wanted to suck smoke into their lungs; in the mornings you could hear soldiers coughing and retching; sometimes the Germans picked up the sound and lobbed a few mortars into the trench.

'I asked you a question young man.'

'A message? Of course I have a message. We're giving the Fritzes a run for their money.'

'He means, of course,' intoned the anonymous voice in the background, 'that we're going to smash them. Chase them out of the Soviet Union all the way back to Berlin.'

The emphasis was always on driving the Germans out of Russia. As though their intrusion was worse than the destruction they had wreaked, the misery they had inflicted.

Gunfire erupted on the west bank, calling him back. Other soldiers had reported that, after a few days of convalescence, they yearned to get back to the fight; as Chuikov had implied it became a habit, the sharing and the killing.

Why bother to ask him questions when the voice in the background answered them for him? The voice was faintly familiar. He turned. Pokrovsky, in the act of rubbing one pointed ear, smiled at him.

'How long will it take you to kill Meister?'

'I've answered that already.' He had already acquired the serviceman's faint contempt for the civilian.

'Do you know anything about him? Education, background, family?'

'Only what I've read translated from *Signal*.'

'What will your feelings be when you kill him? Isn't he very

53

similar to you?' It was the woman with the enormous breasts again.

Pokrovsky said: 'Pride that he has struck a blow against Fascism.'

'Have you and Meister had any exchanges yet?'

'One or two.'

'Close calls?'

'Very.' *Like nearly having my head shot off outside the toy factory.*

'Does Yury write regularly to you?' the reporter with the bunchy hair asked Tasya.

'Every week,' she lied.

'And you to him?'

'Sometimes twice a week.'

Tasya, who hadn't written to him since he arrived in Stalingrad, smiled at him blandly.

A few questions later Pokrovsky called a halt. 'I think,' he announced, 'that these two young people would like to be alone.'

Knowing smiles.

When the journalists had gone Pokrovsky said: 'The house is yours. You have two hours.'

He winked.

***

On the table in the bedroom stood a bottle of pink champagne, Tsimlyanskoye, and two glasses.

Antonov levered off the cork with his thumb; it hit the ceiling and he lost a quarter of the bottle in a gush of pink foam. They laughed, clinked glasses and sipped the champagne; Antonov had never tasted it before; it tasted like cherryade, disappointing.

He glanced at his watch. 'So we have one hour and three-quarters left.'

She stared into her glass. Then: 'Everything's different in war, isn't it. Before the war we would never have thought about this,' glancing at the double bed with the coverlet

54

drawn back. 'Well, we might have thought about it but . . . '

He had thought about it all right: Antonov remembered his imagination slavering the morning after the Komsomol meeting, the morning they had come for him. He had been ashamed of the fertility of his imagination, a perplexing combination of farmyard knowledge and chivalrous respect. But since then he had heard the crude way soldiers referred to women; at first it had shocked him; no longer; however crude their language they still kept creased photographs of wives and girlfriends in their wallets and if anyone made a suggestive remark about those then beware . . . Look what happened to the Muscovite at Akhtubinsk.

Antonov watched the bubbles exploding on the surface of his champagne: he finished the glass, replenished it; the exploding bubbles synchronised with the gunfire on the other side of the river. He gazed speculatively at Tasya, knowing what was expected of him.

'How old are you?' he asked.

'Just eighteen. You know that.'

He felt no desire. This worried him: he had no intention of making love to her – their situation was too contrived – but surely he should have been aroused. He recalled a joke he had heard in the trenches about a Ukrainian – they had a reputation for being henpecked – who couldn't achieve an erection unless he was wearing an apron.

Antonov look a long pull on his champagne.

Tasya kissed him under the ear. 'Don't drink too much,' she said. 'I won't be long.' And then, picking up a blue case, disappeared into the bathroom. He heard the bolt slide home.

Antonov patrolled the lavender-scented room, agonising about his indifference. Panicking about an act that he wasn't going to perform. Stupid!

When she emerged from the bathroom wearing a filmy white nightdress he began to tremble. 'I've left the hot water running for you,' she said and he went into the bathroom carrying his glass of champagne. When he took a swallow the bubbles frothed noisily in his mouth.

Bath towel round his waist, he re-emerged. She was curled

up beneath the sheets, eyes wide open; she had removed her make-up and she reminded him of a child waiting for a bed-time story.

He decided to slip into the bed and kiss her and perhaps caress her and explain that he didn't want to make love because they had both been pushed into it although, God knows, he wanted to, and yes, one day, when they weren't being manipulated, they would make love and it would be wonderful. And he would continue his agonising when she had gone.

But when he got into bed he discovered that there was no need to agonise ever again.

CHAPTER SEVEN

The journey from the west bank of the river to the east had been relatively uneventful; the return trip made up for it.

They departed at Crossing 62 at dusk when, according to the pundits of whom there was no shortage, the German gunners took a break because visibility was confused and it wasn't dark enough for flares. The experts were right until the ferry was half way across.

The flares went up first, rekindling daylight, followed by mortars that sent gouts of water over the bows of the ferry, a dowager, with a tall funnel.

Antonov, sitting in the stern beside a political commissar with soap-shined cheeks and vodka breath, remembered the ships he had seen blown out of the water. Bodies had splashed into the water among the debris. In early September the *Borodino*, with 1,000 wounded soldiers on board, and the *Yosif Stalin*, carrying a similar number of civilian refugees, had been sunk.

Soldiers following the passage of a ship under fire took bets on its chances of reaching its destination.

A yellow flare lit the sky.

'Do you think they're looking for you?' the commissar asked.

Antonov, regarding him with astonishment, saw the features of a man schooled never to accept anything straightforward; the face, he realised at this burgeoning time of awareness, of someone who would never understand that a subtlety of life is sometimes the obvious.

'They don't want me to die here,' he told the commissar. 'They want Meister to get me. If they heard in Berlin that I had been killed by a mortar heads would roll.'

'I suppose you're right.' The commissar rubbed his shiny cheeks with the tips of his fingers. 'What's it like to be so important?'

Antonov glanced at him again; he had the naked air of someone accustomed to wearing spectacles. Without them he was divested of importance. 'Where are your glasses?' he asked.

'I trod on them,' the commissar said.

'Bad luck.' Authority was reaching him every day, but from where he knew not.

'Oh yes, it was bad luck all right.' The commissar peered at the advancing bank of the river.

A mortar engulfed them with water so that, for a long moment, Antonov thought they had been thrown into the river. But when they surfaced they were still sitting on the wooden benches where workers and trippers and lovers, parents and children asking when they were going to reach the other side, had once sat.

Troops crammed on to the slatted benches stared at them curiously.

A dripping soldier said: 'Who are you with?'

Antonov told him.

'So you've been in Stalingrad?'

'A couple of weeks.'

'Is it always like this?' as another mortar showered them with water.

'Always. Who are you with?'

'One hundred and thirty-eighth division. Lyudnikov's mob. The rearguard.'

'Glad to have you on board.' Antonov grinned despite everything.

The mortars stopped firing.

'Shit,' said a voice. 'Here it comes.' As machine-gun bullets ripped through the compressed bodies. But no one had warned the newcomers from Lyudnikov's 138th and the bullets hit them at shoulder level.

Crouching, watching blood mingle with water on the deck in the false daylight, Antonov felt the beginnings of panic ripple through the troops: they had been prepared to fight in the streets but not to be floating targets. In pamphlets handed out as they boarded the ferry they had been advised to hit the ground and make for the nearest cover. Here, the only escape was the river.

The commissar and other political officers, pistols drawn, had taken up positions on the rails. One was shouting through a megaphone: 'Keep calm, another fifty metres and they can't touch us.'

Which was true: when a ship got within a certain distance of the steep shoreline the Germans couldn't bring their guns to bear on it. Antonov had watched this happen and heard soldiers on the shore who had won their bets cheer. But fifty metres was a long way under fire and a MG 34 could fire a lot of bullets in that distance.

The machine-gun opened up again. Men whimpered. Russian big guns on the east bank began to fire, the shells slithering overhead before exploding somewhere in the gathering darkness. To the west the sky was a gentle violet, everywhere else it was brilliant.

A soldier tried to climb onto the rail but a political officer pulled him back. 'Keep calm, not much further – '

Bullets cut through the soldiers again. You could hear their impact on flesh and bone and now some of them were screaming and trying to fight their way to the rail. One political officer fired his pistol into the air.

'Don't panic, only twenty metres – '

Another flare, white this time, lit the sky. A banner of sparks flowed from the funnel of the ferry. Fluorescent feathers of water reared to the starboard as the machine-gun overshot. But the gunner soon corrected his aim: a few feathers rose to the port, then the bullets were among the men again.

Antonov turned to the soldier from Lyudnikov's 138th. 'They're right,' he said. 'A few more metres and we're safe.' But the soldier didn't reply; blood trickled from his mouth and his eyes were closed. He looked like a man who had grown up in the country, Antonov decided; perhaps he was a Siberian who had dreamed of a wooden cottage in the snow-quiet taiga; reassuringly, Antonov patted the dead man's shoulder.

At the rails the political officers were fighting with soldiers trying to jump. Antonov watched with dispassionate interest. Why did they bother? The men were only taking evasive action, adapting the instruction in the pamphlets.

Only a few more metres. Another burst of bullets tore into the bows of the ferry. Lower this time, entering between the lower rail and the deck, ploughing through the mêlée of legs; but even when they were hit the men didn't fall, such was the congestion.

One man was standing on the rail now. The commissar grabbed his legs but the soldier kicked him in the face and dived and by this time two more were on the rails; one jumped, one fell back as a political officer seized one of his legs. Other soldiers climbed on to the rails, rolling, jumping, diving into the water; through the rails Antonov saw them threshing, sinking, surfacing.

He saw the commissar level his pistol at the frantic figures in the water. Impossible. The enemy was over there, finger on the trigger of an MG 34. 'We're all Russians,' he wanted to shout but his lips were frozen, tongue paralysed.

He saw the pistol jerk in the commissar's hand. He gazed into the crowded water. It was turning pink. He looked up again. The commissar was still firing; so were the other political officers. And when a soldier on the deck thrust his way through the bodies and hurled himself at one of them another shot him in the head and kept his pistol levelled at the rest of them.

Suddenly the machine-gun stopped firing; the ferry had reached the shelter of the cliffs. The pistols continued to fire for a few seconds, then they stopped.

The political officers stared at their guns. The men stared at the political officers. Antonov heard the slap of small waves against the hull of the ferry. He screamed but no sound issued from his throat.

***

What will your feeling be when you kill him?

Antonov, sitting in the tunnel, stared at Razin who was feeding his rat with peanuts.

Antonov wasn't sure that he wanted to kill Meister: he would rather have shot the commissar with the soap-shiny cheeks.

CHAPTER EIGHT

'I've only got one piece of advice for you – don't marry a girl unless you laugh at the same things.'

'What if you haven't got any sense of humour?'

'Don't get married at all.'

Meister, hearing his father's voice, smiled and Lanz, zipped into a sleeping bag on Platform One in the Central Railway Station, asked: 'Was she good?'

'Was who good?' Meister stirred sleepily in his bag.

'The girl you were dreaming about.'

'I was dreaming about my father.' A quirky dream because humour wasn't his strong suit.

Meister shielded his eyes against the dawn light shining through the space where the roof had been, then closed them and tried to summon his father back to the dream.

After a while he returned but now he was a clown in a circus and other clowns were pouring water over him, bucket after bucket of it, and the white paint was being washed from his face and the water streaming down his cheeks was tears and the spectators laughing at his discomfort were all Jews and Meister found that he, too, was laughing. And crying.

And, watched by his mother holding a parasol, he was flying a kite, a dragon with a green tail, on the clipped grass on the banks of the Aussenalster. At first the kite wouldn't leave the ground; then his father, pointed beard wagging, made an adjustment to the tail and the kite took off taking Meister with it,

When he let go he fell towards the lake but a gust of wind blew him towards the Historical Museum to the south-west of Hamburg and he tumbled into an old-fashioned rifle range. He peered along the barrel of a musket and, beyond the primitive sights, saw Antonov, but when he squeezed the trigger he disappeared in a puff of smoke.

Meister awoke with a jerk.

Lanz, squatting on his sleeping bag peeling an apple, said: 'You dreamt you were falling? When you hit the ground you're dead.'

Meister sat up and looked round the shell of the station. Sleeping soldiers lay on the platforms and the concourse; a black locomotive lay on its side – as though it had been slapped; the station clock had stopped at 4.20; the stalls in the men's lavatory stood exposed; a crooked nameplate at the end of the platform where he and Lanz were camped indicated that a train had once stood there panting, waiting to depart for Rostov – Meister wondered if it had got there. The station had changed hands many times in the early days of the battle, five times in one morning, and there were dark stains on the concrete between the two sleeping bags.

A German spotter plane, the daily prelude to hostilities, droned across the sky, its pilot looking for Soviet re-inforcements that had crossed the Volga overnight. As soon as the pilot radioed back to base Junkers and Heinkels would take off, heavy with bombs.

Lanz said, 'How did your father make his money?'

Not *what sort of a father was he?* A thief knew his priorities. 'Perfume,' he said.

At least he had succeeded in surprising Lanz. 'Perfume?' Lanz placed his fingers on his skull-cap baldness and rubbed the flesh backwards and forwards on the bone. 'You mean we still made perfume while we were re-arming?'

'You'd be surprised how much we produced.' He could hear his father telling him how much. Felt the scratch of his grey-threaded beard against his cheek as he kissed him goodnight and turned his face away from his cigar-smell.

63

'I hope you didn't wear it.'

'No, but the whole house smelled of it. My father used to bring samples home from the factory and ask my mother to give her opinion. Then she gave them to the maids and they swamped themselves with it.'

'Maids! National Socialism was all right for some.' Lanz chewed the core of the apple, then ate the skin. Why had he bothered to peel it? 'Is your old man a member of the Party?'

The question invited an apology and Meister was grateful to the Russian gunners who opened up on the other side of the river making conversation impossible for the moment.

His father was a Party member and many of Hamburg's leading Nazis had visited the tall, gabled house in the centre of the city. From his bedroom Meister had heard the murmur of dinner conversation, rising in volume as the meal progressed, and the toasts to the Führer and, occasionally, martial songs, although these were muted and short-lived when his mother, purveyor of unspoken but aristocratic reproof, was present.

Once or twice Goebbels had been present. Small, lame, unprepossessing, he had become transformed when he spoke, words like cascading stars lighting the future.

Before dinner, while drinks were being served in front of the log fire, Goebbels, still in uniform after the Party rally, swastika on his arm, had talked to Meister.

'And how do you propose to serve the Fatherland?' he had asked.

Meister, fifteen at the time, determined only that he wanted nothing to do with perfume, told him that he hadn't made up his mind.

'Do you enjoy reading and writing? Theatre, cinema? Do you read the newspapers?'

Meister answered affirmatively although the scope of the questions made total honesty elusive. He told Goebbels that he had written an essay about the years of waste after the Treaty of Versailles.

'I'd like to see it. Maybe I'll find a job for you one day.' Goebbels smiled conspiratorially; on the other side of the fire his father gazed at them speculatively. 'It's been said before –

"The pen is mightier than the sword" – but never forget that it's words not bullets that win wars.'

At the time that had sounded neat and wise and Meister might have joined Dr. Goebbels' propaganda machine if he hadn't won a trophy involving bullets instead of words.

That night, after the guests had departed, wives carrying gifts of perfume, his father, breath smelling of violet cachous, had come to his bedroom and questioned him about his conversation with Goebbels.

'So, what did the good doctor have to say?'

Meister told him.

'Was that all?'

Sleepily, he tried to remember if Goebbels had let slip any other pearls of wisdom; he couldn't understand why his father wanted to know.

'He seemed quite happy with everything here?'

'Quite happy, Papa.'

'Did he mention me?' voice suddenly very casual.

'Not once.' Meister yawned.

'That's all right then.' He couldn't tell whether his father was pleased or disappointed. 'A very able man, Dr. Goebbels. Even though he doesn't come from very good stock.'

As the big guns stopped firing, leaving a buzzing in Meister's ears, a soldier on a bicycle pedalled onto the platform. 'For you.' He handed Meister an envelope. 'Lucky bastard, I haven't had a letter for weeks.'

'You're not a star turn,' Lanz told him.

Meister glanced at the envelope. Elzbeth's businesslike writing. He ripped it open.

'I'll get some coffee,' Lanz said.

Dearest Karl,

I love you and miss you and think about you all the time. As if she wanted to get the formalities over and done with. *And perhaps it won't be long until we are together as we read in the newspapers that Stalingrad is on the point of surrender*. Did she really believe that or was one of Goebbels' minions standing behind her? *You have become quite a celebrity here and we're all very proud of you and all the other girls are very jealous of me*. No, this wasn't Elzbeth; by now the real Elzbeth would have cut him down to size. *They – who? – tell me that when Stalingrad falls you will be allowed leave. And who knows, a decoration?*

Meister folded the letter and replaced it in the envelope because there was no point in finishing it: Elzbeth, who didn't even know of Antonov's existence, was being used to urge him to finish the job.

Lanz returned with some foul coffee and a tin of corned beef he had found under a pile of rubble in the refreshment room.

'Well,' he asked, 'how's everything back home?'

'Ticking over. How's the battle?' Lanz always returned from foraging missions with the latest news of the fighting.

'We're still winning. Surprising how long it's taking considering we're winning every day. We've taken the Tractor Plant and cut the Russians in two *again* and we're within 400 yards of the river between the Barricade and Red October factories. God knows, we might even advance another couple of yards today.' He opened the tin of corned beef with a clasp-knife. 'Everyone wants to know when you're going to kill Antonov.'

'Soon.'

'Take your time.' Lanz handed him half the tin of meat.

'The trouble is we anticipate each other all the time.'

'You anticipated him in front of the toy factory?'

'He anticipated me.'

'You should have shot his head off.' Lanz ate a mouthful of meat from the blade of his knife.

'We've got to find fresh cover. Antonov knows about the factory.'

'A cemetery?'

At that moment Misha arrived. It was the second time he had visited them.

He had brought a bucket of water, raw potatoes and a cucumber. He told Meister who had taken Russian at college that he had the latest dispositions of the Soviet troops to pass on to 6th Army headquarters. The Russians, he said, were in a desperate position in the industrial north: one more push and Paulus could claim victory.

'If we had the reserves to push with,' Lanz said when Meister translated.

'The Germans are within a few hundred yards of Chuikov's headquarters,' Misha said.

'Then what's stopping them from taking it?' Meister asked and Lanz, getting the gist, said: 'Russians.'

Lanz poured water into his mess-tin and drank from it, spilling some on his grey-green tunic, carefully wiping a drop from his Iron Cross. He said to Meister: 'Ask him why he's so anxious to help the Germans?'

'Why not?' Misha protested. 'They're winning.'

'No one is as callous as that,' Lanz said. 'Not even me.'

'All right,' Misha said to Meister, 'the Russians took my father to Siberia. I never saw him again. My mother cried every night. Would you want the Russians to win?'

'Ask him why they took his father,' Lanz said.

'He doesn't really know,' Meister said when the boy had finished. 'His father was in the army. It's possible, the purges . . .'

'I think he's a liar,' Lanz said. 'It takes one to spot one. Ask him if he knows of a good place to hole up before we go looking for Antonov again.'

Misha smiled and the war left his face. Meister noticed that he had one tooth missing; it made him momentarily defenceless. He also had a graze on one knee – there had never been a time in Meister's own childhood when one of his knees hadn't been grazed – and burrs on the socks collapsed round his ankles.

'I know just the place,' he told Meister.

They walked warily through the ruined streets in the direction of Tsaritsa Gorge, the 200-foot deep ravine where the Soviet headquarters had been earlier in the campaign.

Lanz, pistol drawn, suspecting a trap, walked beside the boy: Russian civilians, in radio communication with the military, were still used to lure Germans down streets covered by Soviet gunners: when the guns opened up the civilians disappeared into the subterranean depths of the city.

A cold wind had sprung up but it didn't disperse the smell of rotting corpses.

'It will snow soon,' Misha said. 'And that will help the Russians. You must be quick.' As he talked he nibbled sunflower seeds, cracking the husks with his teeth and dropping them on the ground.

They passed sagging signs offering cherry jam and apples for sale and picked their way along ruptured tracks where shabby trams had once run. Finally they came to a shell-torn wall. 'Here,' Misha said.

They went behind the wall. 'It was my school,' he said.

Of the school there was nothing left except the shell of a classroom containing crippled desks and chairs and a wall-clock lying on its back but still working. Its fluttering hands pointed at 12.30 but they were wrong.

The playground, a square of punished grass and frozen mud, was untouched by debris.

Meister took off his steel helmet and walked round the square. One patch of turf was completely bald – 'That used to be the goal,' Misha explained – and in a corner stood a pear tree, a couple of withered fruit hanging from its branches.

'Every kid's dream,' Lanz said, 'to have his school demolished.' He had put a chair on the grass and was sitting smoking a cigarette. 'I wonder why he was lying.'

'Maybe he wasn't.' Meister sat on the grass. It was like holy ground; even the gunfire seemed distant, the accompaniment to someone else's battle. He plucked a blade of grass and nibbled the cold stalk.

Lanz fished in the breast pocket of his tunic and produced a soiled sugar almond – Lanz's pockets were lucky dips. He handed it to the boy; Misha, sitting under the pear tree, sucked it experimentally.

Lanz said: 'Ask him if he knows about Antonov.'

68

Misha said he did, everyone did.

'Ask him if he knows you're Meister?'

'Of course,' Misha said, cracking the sugared almond with his teeth, surprised at the question.

'Do you think he'll kill me?' Meister asked.

'It depends.'

'On what?'

Somewhere a dog barked, a lonely sound in the chilled sunlight. A rifle shot and the barking stopped.

'We had a dog,' Misha said. 'It was called Druzhok. It disappeared in the fighting.'

'Ask him where his mother is,' Lanz instructed Meister.

Misha jerked his thumb downwards and spoke rapidly.

'I think,' Meister told Lanz, 'that she's hiding in a cellar or a sewer. Apparently there are thousands of refugees underground.'

'Does she know what he's doing?'

'Does it matter?'

'I just don't believe a kid like that would want to help us.'

'A lot of Ukrainians joined us.'

'That was before Kiev. Then they fought us with only five bullets apiece, fought with Stalin's voice booming over the loudspeakers. And when they had used their five bullets they still fought.'

'Were you there?' Meister was curious about Lanz's Iron Cross but the thief never discussed it.

'I've been everywhere.' Lanz pinched out his cigarette. 'Ask him where Antonov's hiding.'

Misha was wandering about the wrecked schoolroom poking about in the debris. He found a grey exercise book and riffled the pages. They were filled with crayoned drawings, children with beetroot faces, ships on pointed waves, bears with huge paws, all beneath strips of blue sky.

'I asked you a question,' Meister said.

'I don't know where he is.'

'He's lying,' Lanz said.

'You think everyone's lying.'

'Even to themselves. Ask him again.'

The boy turned his back and stared at the clock.

'He knows,' Lanz said. He delved into one of the lower pockets of his tunic.

What now? A white rabbit?

The gold watch lay in the shiny palm of Lanz's hand imprisoning the sunlight. Lanz called Misha's name. 'Look.' He swung the watch on its chain. 'Come here.' He beckoned with his other hand. 'Listen.' After a moment the watch chimed, a tiny silver noise inside the gold. 'Tell him he can have it if he tells us where Antonov is.'

Meister hesitated.

'What's the matter? You want Antonov to find you?'

'I don't like using the boy.'

'A sniper with a conscience! Jesus Christ!'

Lanz turned to the boy. Dangled the watch. Pointed at it and pointed at Misha. 'Antonov?' he asked.

The watch swung like a pendulum.

The boy's eyes moved from side to side.

'Antonov?'

Misha stretched out one hand.

Lanz withdrew the watch.

'Antonov?'

The boy swallowed.

Very slowly, Lanz moved the watch towards his tunic pocket.

Misha told Meister that Antonov was hiding in a sewer on the banks of the Volga.

CHAPTER NINE

Later that morning Meister was summoned to the presence of Paulus who was conferring with his commanders at 6th Army headquarters, a cluster of farm buildings at Golubinskaya, forty miles west of Stalingrad on the banks of another river, the Don.

But the general was alone, warming his back in front of a log fire in the farmhouse overlooking a mutilated cornfield, when Meister arrived. He looked older and Meister who until now hadn't considered subtleties of age – only young, old and very old – couldn't quite make out where it showed.

Paulus, theatrically spruce – he was said to wear gloves on the battlefield – was absent-mindedly tapping a cigarette on a silver case when Meister entered the room. He stared at Meister and through him, a tic fluttering beneath one eye. Eventually Paulus told him to stand at ease.

He lit the cigarette and turned to warm his hands and Meister got the fleeting impression that he was preparing himself for winter because it wasn't that cold. Winter . . . They were supposed to have taken Stalingrad in August!

Meister glanced at the table separating him from Paulus. There was a bottle of schnapps on it, Korn, and an ashtray heaped with cigarette butts and yet another map scored with arrowheads; but these arrowheads, probing from the south and the north had question marks beside them and suddenly Meister realised they were Russian.

'So, what do you think?' Paulus asked, noticing that he was studying the map.

Think? Think about what? Ah, the map 'Is this where you think the Russians will try and counter-attack, Herr General?' It hadn't occurred to him that the Russians had a counter-attack left in them.

'It's a possibility. And if they do . . .'

Paulus didn't elaborate. The pouch under one eye quivered. Why should a general discuss tactics with a soldier? Thinking aloud probably. Debating possibilities that he couldn't broach with officers? It was a flattering proposition.

'It's getting cold,' Paulus said. 'Soon it will snow. The Russians love snow – it's their ammunition.'

Meister said nothing because no reply had been invited but a word that he had considered fluttered like a snowflake into his consciousness. DEFEAT. But that was preposterous.

'At first,' Paulus said, 'cold is good. It freezes the mud and we can move our trucks and guns. But that's only cold as we understand it: it isn't Russian cold. When the Russian cold makes its début the earth becomes concrete three feet deep and the wind blows the temperature down to minus forty and soldiers wear anything to keep it at bay, even towels and bedclothes, but even then, they lose their arms and legs and when a horse is frostbitten to death there's a celebration because there's meat to eat. I only know,' Paulus said, 'because I had a friend at Moscow.'

A half-track trundled past the window on the rutted road. Between the pink and blue fretted eaves of the farmhouse it looked as though it were crossing a stage. 'Re-inforcements,' said Paulus; Meister detected a sardonic note.

Paulus kicked a log with the toe of one polished boot; ash fell softly, a strip of bark caught fire.

'Tell me, Meister, is this how you envisaged the war?'

'No, Herr General.'

'How then?'

'Just victories. Like Poland and France. Stupid of me, I suppose.'

'Not so stupid,' Paulus said. 'It was what you were brought

up to believe. What do you think went wrong?'

'Nothing I suppose. Things had to get tougher.'

'Before final victory?'

'Before final victory, Herr General.'

'And you've never doubted the final outcome?'

'Never, Herr General.' *Not until now*.

'The Führer is a great man.'

Meister nodded.

'Without him we would still be nothing. The Thousand Year Reich, an inspired concept.'

Meister could find nothing to add to that.

'If only we had the reserves . . . Do you know you're an old man, Meister? They're sending us seventeen-year-olds now. Children.'

'I've heard,' Meister ventured, 'that the Soviets have brought in tailors and cobblers, sailors even, to fight here.'

'And fight they will,' Paulus said. 'Like animals defending their young, dying with snarls frozen on their faces.' He lit another cigarette; his hands shook. 'So when do you propose to kill Antonov?'

'As soon as possible, Herr General.'

'Not soon enough. I had a message this morning from the Führer in Bavaria. He can't understand why you're taking so long.'

'Because Antonov is good.'

'Better than you?'

'The same.'

'Have you taken a shot at him yet?'

'One,' Meister admitted.

'And you missed?' Paulus was incredulous.

Meister explained about the smoke.

'Has he taken a shot at you?'

'It's his turn, Herr General.'

'Then we must pray for more smoke. After that it will be your turn again, Meister, and this time you mustn't miss. Understand? Because I'm not concerned any longer about the people back home, the Press, the radio, I'm concerned about my troops staring into winter. They need your victory:

73

that's worth more than a battalion of re-inforcements. If you killed Antonov today they'd take what's left of this God-forsaken city tomorrow.'

'I'll do my best, Herr General.'

'Good.' With one finger Paulus tried to arrest the tic beneath his eye. 'And then perhaps we shall be able to turn our attention to those arrows,' pointing at the map on the table.

To Meister it seemed as though the arrows had become sharper but that, of course, was his imagination.

***

The motor-cycle and sidecar taking Meister back to the centre of Stalingrad stopped in a hamlet a mile down the road. Wooden cottages with mossy roofs, picket fences, a log road leading to a square with a water-pump in the middle.

The scaffold was also made of wood.

The motor-cyclist, young with acne-scarred cheeks, said: 'It looks as if we're going to have some fun'.

Meister, steel helmet cradled in his lap, peered out of the sidecar. Soldiers armed with rifles were posted round the square; near the scaffold stood a group of peasants, women wearing headscarves, men peaked caps or fur hats with spaniel ears. They seemed indifferent to their fate, as though suffering were a fifth season of the year.

'What the hell's going on?' he asked the motor-cyclist.

'Wait and see. But I can tell you this – these bastards are lucky. When partisans blew up a bridge near Sevastopol we burned down a whole village and shot anyone who tried to escape.'

Meister who had heard such stories and dismissed them as the fictions of war said: 'Did you actually see this happen?' and when the motor-cyclist admitted that he hadn't, allowed himself a mature and indulgent smile.

A cold, mud-smelling breeze nosed its way into the square. Away to the east castles of cloud were assembling. The peasants remained mute, motionless, garbed with forlorn dignity.

'Look,' the motor-cyclist pointed down the log road on the opposite side of the square. Meister saw a youth and a girl approaching; their hands were tied behind their backs and hanging from the youth's neck was a placard: WE ARE PARTISANS AND WE HAVE KILLED GERMAN SOLDIERS. AS WE ARE CIVILIANS WE KNOW WE MUST PAY THE PENALTY. Behind them walked two German soldiers and an officer brandishing a pistol; with his long greatcoat and boots and shiny-peaked cap he cut quite a figure.

A corporal wearing steel-rimmed glasses and a forage cap that was too small for him slung two ropes over the cross-piece of the gallows, made them secure and tied two nooses. Then he rubbed his hands together, a man who knew his job and liked appreciation.

Meister noticed two children in the silent group. A small boy with ragged trousers flapping round his shins and a girl of about twelve wearing a white shawl. The boy held the girl's hand. Meister saw trust flowing between them; their parents had been killed; he *knew* that.

He wanted to leave the square but he had to stay in case it didn't happen. In case humanity was given a reprieve.

The ropes, braided red and white, looked like bell-ropes from a church.

Meister turned to look at the youth and the girl approaching the gallows. They, too, looked like brother and sister. Her hair was cropped, figure boyish; she reminded Meister of Joan of Arc. The boy wore a big, white cap with a small peak protruding from beneath it; he wore it at a jaunty angle, smiling with tremulous ferocity. The girl stared ahead expressionlessly.

Meister was amazed at their composure. Their lives were about to be switched off. No world. Nothing. And they're younger than me. Meister searched their faces for their childhood and saw his own and smelled perfume. His hand went to his throat; he hoped they believed in God.

The officer pulled the ropes with gloved hands, testing them.

Meister concentrated on the youth's cap. He must have been very proud of that cap when he bought it.

The girl's lips were moving. Praying? The boy's smile broke into fragments, re-assembled fiercer than ever.

The cap. Look at the cap. Perhaps he had kept his money in it. Taken it off with a flourish, produced a soiled rouble note and bought his first girl a rose with silver paper round the stem.

The cap. Concentrate on the cap. He had probably experimented with it, turned it back to front and imagined himself at the wheel of an open tourer.

The cap fell to the ground and on the breeze funnelled along the log road where the boy and girl had just walked the smell of perfume was strong.

CHAPTER TEN

The rain came from the east, a last cleansing before winter. Scattered drops at first that coaxed dry scents from the dust and rubble; then a sustained drizzle reaching back into Siberia.

Antonov, crouching with Razin in a shell hole near the Barricade gun factory, smiled at the coldness of it on his cheeks. Very soon now it would turn to snow.

All morning they had hunted Meister but, with nine-tenths of the city in enemy hands, the German had the advantage, free to wander the yawning acres of devastation and concentrate on the Russian pocket in the north – unless one of the civilian storm squads operating in the ruins got him.

By early afternoon Antonov had decided that the best strategy was to wait for Meister to come for him and, with Razin's assistance, he devised a trap. When they knew Meister was close Razin would raise his helmet on the end of a stick; if Meister put a bullet through it Razin would rear up screaming; Meister would show himself and Antonov would shoot him.

It was, they acknowledged, a hackneyed ploy – and Antonov had seen it in a silent film about the Civil War – but, with their backs to the Volga and the stricken factories where the Soviet pocket had been cut in two, there was no scope for originality.

They wore rubber capes but the rain found its way inside

them and Razin worried about his lungs which, he insisted, had been weak since an attack of pleurisy in his childhood. From time to time he coughed discreetly but irritatingly, in fact Antonov found that the cough, and the soft tap of rain on his helmet, were more distracting than the thunder of battle a few hundred yards away. After a while he took off his helmet and put on his forage cap; it quickly became sodden.

'You'll catch a cold in the head,' Razin told him.

Antonov shook his dripping head. 'We don't get colds in the head where I come from.'

'Spoken like a true Siberian? You know something? You Siberians are a pain in the ass.'

'Siberians saved Stalingrad.'

'According to *Red Star* Rodimtsev and the 13th Guards saved Stalingrad.'

'They fought well. But so did Zholudev's 37th and Gorishny's 95th and all the others.'

Sometimes Antonov felt wiser than Razin; this dated from the night he had returned from the east bank of the Volga.

'And the 112th. What about them?' Razin demanded. 'They fought like demons but they haven't been given Guards status. Why? Because they're hooligans, criminals, that's why. Worse, political agitators – the worst crime in the penal code. No, they won't get any medals: doubters can't be heroes.' He brushed a drop of rainwater from his sagging moustache. 'Have you ever doubted?'

Doubted? Razin made belief sound shameful. What he didn't understand, or had forgotten, or had never known, was that in childhood doubt doesn't arise, trust prevails. What is there to doubt? He wanted to explain this to Razin but instead he said: 'Yes, I've doubted,' although the doubt had only been with him for a few days.

'Doubted what?'

'Values.'

'Did you know that when the Germans first attacked Russia our army was run by a bunch of amateurs because Stalin had purged all the professionals? And when I say purged I mean shot. They say he got rid of 35,000 commanders.'

'You expect me to believe that?'

Razin shrugged. 'I don't care what you believe. But I do know that the greatest crime is naïvety.'

A Russian 50 mm mortar opened up. Antonov waited for the explosion in the German lines, wondering if he could distinguish it from the all-encompassing din of battle. At first the noise had sent needles of pain shooting through his skull; now he was indifferent to it, although at dawn, before the daily bombardment began, his head ached. A heap of bricks erupted where the mortar shell had fallen, but he couldn't identify the explosion.

Razin said: 'You must have heard how the peasants were massacred because they didn't want to work on collective farms?'

Only whispers over the vodka bottle when his father entertained. But they had contained little substance and he had bracketed them with jests which took on an uncharacteristic coarseness half way down the bottle.

No, the only injustice with which he had been regaled by his teacher, who always wore black and combed her hair into a polished bun that looked like a doorknob, had been the tyranny of the Czars until Lenin and then Koba, the Indomitable, Stalin, had come to the rescue of the downtrodden masses.

'Millions died,' Razin said.

'Why are you telling me this?'

'So that you know what you're fighting for.'

'For peace,' Antonov said.

'Cosy.'

'What are you fighting for?'

'What might have been.'

'You're fighting because you're a Russian,' Antonov said. 'Just like the other Ukrainians you told me about.'

Razin smiled his yellow smile. 'That too.'

Another mortar shell exploded, closer this time. Antonov wiped the lenses of his field-glasses with a handkerchief and peered over the rim of the crater. A German Panzer III tank was approaching, a prehistoric monster foraging uncertainly

79

in another age, so any moment now Russian PTRS anti-tank rifles would be barking. Through the field-glasses Antonov saw a Death's Head on the tank's turret.

He swivelled the glasses and gazed at the remains of a small house, staircase still clinging to a green-painted wall. He imagined generations of a family climbing those stairs, children's fingers trailing on the green paint as they raced down them, early for play or late for school. A movement. As slight as a blink but positive. A rat, a cat, a wounded man, a sniper . . . He handed the field-glasses to Razin. 'Can you see anything?'

Razin concentrated on the ruin. Then: 'You know what I think?'

'Meister?'

'Who else would be holed up in No Man's Land opposite our crater?'

The rain thickened. Water streamed off Razin's helmet veiling his face.

The Panzer III turned and headed for the crater.

Razin said: 'Look at it this way. Either he,' pointing at the ruined house, 'gets us or,' pointing at the tank, 'we get crushed by that or,' tapping his chest, 'we die of pneumonia.'

'The trap.' Antonov wasn't as enthusiastic as he should have been. 'Here, use my helmet.'

Razin balanced the helmet on the end of a length of picket-fence, and Antonov thought: 'This isn't the way it should end.'

'Ready?'

Antonov nodded.

'Got bullets in that thing?' pointing at the Mosin-Nagant.

Antonov shook his head.

'You should be a comedian.' Razin raised the helmet over the lip of the crater and the crack came immediately and the helmet leapt from his perch splashing into the puddle in the bottom of the crater, and Razin was rearing up screaming and Antonov, gun-butt pushing into his shoulder, was peering through the telescopic sights at the house and hoping that no one would fall for such an elementary ruse but there he was,

80

head and shoulders making a beautiful target, but it was too easy. Stupid, he tried to kill you. He squeezed the trigger knowing that it was the worst shot of his life. The head and shoulders became a body, arms upraised, rifle falling, and above the sound of battle Antonov heard his scream.

Later, when the tank had passed, when the shooting had become sporadic, they made their way to the house. They found him lying beneath the exposed stairs, still alive, the wound in his shoulder instead of between his eyes. For a sniper of Antonov's skill it was a very bad shot; but in a sense that was irrelevant because the wounded man, middle-aged and unshaven, wasn't Meister.

***

The rain was turning to sleet as Antonov and Razin returned in the late afternoon to the tunnel, taking a mine-free route two sappers had shown them. Fires burned in the shells of factories, three Stukas, songsters as the troops called them, made a last sortie over the beleaguered Russians. A corn-cob, a Soviet bomber made of wood, limped back to the east bank, wounded by Messerschmitt 109's or anti-aircraft guns. Fish stunned by shells and bombs floated on the Volga, silver bellies bared to the sleet. Antonov and Razin's long boots sank ankle-deep in new mud.

On an evening such as this the tunnel was home.

It was certainly drier than the world outside and Razin had furnished it with a shabby red carpet, a couple of straw mattresses, mugs and plates, pots and pans, two boxes that had contained rattles – boxes of anti-infantry grenades the Luftwaffe sometimes dropped instead of bombs – a primus stove and a packet of yellow candles. On the wall he had stuck a German leaflet calling on the Russians to lay down their arms.

When they climbed into the tunnel through a shell-hole fifty yards from the riverbank they found a candle had been lit. In its light they saw Misha sitting on one of the mattresses.

81

He was eating sunflower seeds and Boris the rat was watching him keenly.

***

Sketch-map in hand, Lanz led the way through the sleet. 'It's over there somewhere,' he said, pointing in the direction of the Red October Plant. 'At the foot of some shallow cliffs near a stony beach.' He peered at the map on which Misha had marked the site of the tunnel with a red crayon.

They made their way through a park gouged with craters towards the Volga. It wasn't dusk but already there was cruelty, as distinct from the brutality of battle, abroad; Meister could feel it in the sting of the sleet, smell it on the stale scents of distemper and spent explosives, feel it in the gaze of unseen watchers in the ruins. In some countries dusk was known as the time between dog and wolf; in Stalingrad that time was now, a brooding interlude between day and night conflict.

A sentry challenged them from the shadow of a signal box. They gave the password, Pandora, and identified themselves. The sentry, young with a wound cobwebbed with stitches on his cheek, was impressed. 'Are you looking for Antonov?'

'That was the general idea,' Lanz said.

'I hear he's shot a hundred men. How many have you shot?' he asked Meister.

'A hundred and one,' Lanz said. 'What the hell are you guarding here?'

'Regimental headquarters.' The sentry pointed at a group of sheds across the track. 'The Ivans tried to take it this morning. A special squad of fifty NKVD militia. They must have crossed the river overnight.'

'Obviously they failed.'

'But Christ, could they fight. They came at us howling like jackals but we mowed them down with an MG 42. Well, most of them.'

'And the rest?'

'Out there somewhere.'

'Between here and the Red October Plant.'

'I suppose so,' the sentry said. 'That's where you're heading for?'

Meister said it was.

'You're crazy.'

'Better now than in broad daylight.'

'They don't fight like ordinary men. They're . . . ' He searched for the word. ' . . . possessed.'

Lanz said to Meister: 'Sure you want to go ahead?'

'Sure.'

'Don't forget I outrank you.'

'I'm sure Paulus would be interested to hear you were scared of a few fugitives. Hitler too . . . '

'He doesn't want you dead.'

'Which is why you've got to take care of me.'

They left the sentry staring uncertainly at them and made their way into the gathering darkness where the dogs were now wolves.

***

'He *gave* you this?' Razin swung the gold watch on its chain; it had uttered a fragile chime from Misha's pocket and Razin had fished it out.

'In exchange for food.'

'They're hard up for food but not that hard up.'

'Bread,' Misha said. 'Warm bread like the bread I gave you. And a little cheese.'

'Have you got bread for us? Or are we having sunflower seeds?'

'I've got something better,' Misha said. 'A better place to hide.'

'We're not hiding,' Antonov told him.

Misha frowned uncomprehendingly. 'A much better place than this,' as though nothing could be worse.

'Why is it so much better?' Razin asked.

'No rats.' Misha looked at Boris.

'Is that all?'

'It's better placed for killing Meister.'

Misha looked from Razin to Antonov and back again and his face was quick with sharp wisdom.

Razin asked: 'And how could you know that?'

'Because I know where he's hiding.'

Razin looked at Antonov. 'Where?'

'I will show you.'

'Does he know you know?'

Misha shook his head. He threw the rat a husk of a sunflower seek, baked and salted, according to the packet, in Kharkov. The rat grabbed the husk but, finding no sustenance inside, discarded it and, whiskers twitching, continued to follow the boy's movements.

'Where did you meet him?' Razin asked.

'Outside *Univermag*.'

'And you followed him?' Antonov asked.

'Of course.'

'You did well. Here, I can't match the watch but take this.' He handed Misha a two-bladed penknife, its sheath covered with mother-of-pearl.

'There's something wrong,' Razin said.

'What can possibly be wrong?'

'I don't know,' Razin said. 'One gold watch, one penknife, he's doing well . . . '

'I'll use them to buy food,' Misha said. 'And information. Did you know I've met General Chuikov?' He finished the sunflower seeds and stood up. 'Now we must go.'

'To the new place?' Razin lit the primus stove on which their supper, soup made from dried potatoes and bread, stood in a bowl, cold and congealed. 'Not tonight. We've just got here. We'll have a look at it tomorrow.'

A bubble rose from the stagnant depths of the soup and burst on the surface.

Misha pulled his arm. 'No, we must go now.' He was blinking rapidly. He turned to Antonov. 'Please.' His hand on Antonov's arm was a small claw.

Razin, stirring the soup, said: 'What's the hurry? Meister isn't going anywhere. Not on a night like this.'

'Tell him,' Misha said to Antonov.

'Tell him what? Anyway, let's have supper first.' Antonov found some black bread in the rattle box and cut it into two and then into three.

Razin took a swig of home-made vodka he had found in a shed in a devastated vegetable garden. 'We'll take a look in the morning.' His voice sounded suddenly sleepy.

'No,' Misha said. 'Now!'

'You see,' Razin said, 'I knew there was something wrong.' He rolled a pellet of black bread and threw it to the rat.

***

Lanz, consulting the map in the hooded beam of a flashlight, said: 'I think we're close.' His voice was muffled as though it was full of sleet.

They could hear the river close by but they couldn't see it: they hadn't expected it to be so dark. Occasionally German flares burst overhead but even they had lost their dazzle.

Meister slipped his hand beneath his cape and felt the bulge in his tunic pocket. The white cap with the small peak. He intended to give it to the family of the dead boy.

What was Antonov doing now crouched in the tunnel? Writing to his girl? A country girl with a fine skin and white, white teeth. Meister envied him sitting in his tunnel writing to his girl.

Lanz said: 'According to the kid Antonov gets into the tunnel through a shell-hole fifty yards from the river. If it wasn't for that hole he'd be sitting in sewage. I wonder what the hell they do in there?'

'Play chess maybe,' replied Meister who didn't want to share Antonov's letter-writing.

'Anyway it will be dry in there and they won't be expecting us and if you lower yourself through the hole you'll be able to get in a couple of shots before they go for their guns.'

'Maybe,' Meister said.

'Or maybe I should roll a grenade down the tunnel.'

'It's got to be a bullet,' Meister said. 'You know that.' He tapped the Karabiner through the waterproofed webbing.

85

But he wasn't being totally truthful with Lanz.

He stumbled over a body. He couldn't tell whether it was Russian or German.

Lanz gripped his arm, doused the flashlight. They froze. Ahead a movement, a splash of water in a puddle. Lanz's fingers bit into Meister's arm. With his other hand he drew his pistol.

The flare exploded above them, light blurred by the sleet. As a machine-pistol opened up. As Lanz falling to the ground and pulling Meister with him, fired his pistol at the gun-bursts. The shooting stopped. They waited, pressed into the mud.

Lanz crawled forward. Meister slid his rifle from the webbing and covered him. Finally Lanz stood up and beckoned him. He rolled the body over with his foot. 'Secret police,' he said. 'NKVD. Christ, look at that gun.' He picked it up, it looked home-made. 'They must make them in their tool-sheds,' adding: 'Thank Christ.'

'Why "Thank Christ"?'

'Because if they didn't they'd strangle us with their bare hands.'

They moved on in what they hoped was the direction of the tunnel.

***

'We *must* go now,' Misha said. 'We must.'

'When we've finished eating,' Razin said. 'Boris doesn't like to go without his supper. Do you?' He threw the rat another pellet of black bread. 'In any case, what's the hurry?'

'The Fritzes are going to attack this stretch of the river bank at dawn.'

'You wouldn't lie to me would you, Misha?'

'I know about these things.'

Antonov said: 'We'd better do what he says.'

'I don't trust him. Do you?'

'It doesn't matter.' He saw the political officers emptying their pistols into the soldiers floundering in the river. Since then he had adopted a new policy: neither trust nor distrust, neither believe nor disbelieve: it was easier that way. 'But if the Germans do take this stretch of river bank we're trapped.'

Razin wiped his mess-tin clean with a piece of bread which he ate, chewing slowly.

Misha said: 'You won't even get wet, we're going underground.' He pulled at Antonov's sleeve. 'We can get there through the tunnel on the other side of the shell-hole,' pointing into the darkness beyond the candlelight.

Antonov, neither believing or disbelieving, began to pack his gear.

***

'There's the shell-hole,' Lanz whispered. The sleet had eased and Meister could just make out a black wound in the hump of the tunnel.

'Good,' Meister said. 'Now we'll be able to find it easily.'

'What the fuck are you talking about?'

'In the morning,' Meister said, glad at last he could release the deceit. 'At dawn. When we come for him.'

'Don't give me any of that shit,' Lanz said. 'We've come for him now.'

'I can't shoot him down there,' Meister said. 'Not hiding in a sewer.' There was sometimes dignity in death; he had seen it already on the battlefield. 'You don't shoot a man in the back or when he's eating or sleeping.'

'I do.' Lanz drew his pistol.

'No.'

'Try and stop me and you get the first bullet.'

And he was away, swallowed up by the black wound, and Meister was shouting to Antonov in German and broken Russian and he was down in the darkness of the tunnel making for the faint grey orb where the sewer disgorged into the river.

The beam of the flashlight startled him. He watched it explore the rounded walls, pick out some boxes, a couple of mattresses.

Lanz's voice reached him in echoes. 'The little bastard has double-crossed us. He came here and warned them.'

Meister, following the beam of the flashlight, saw a pile of sunflower seed husks on the carpet.

CHAPTER ELEVEN

In the subterranean world of Stalingrad women were in charge. In cellars, sewers and connecting tunnels they shepherded what was left of families – old men, *babushki*, children – into groups where, surrounded by prams, punished chairs and primus stoves, they cooked and clucked and crooned. Sometimes they camped beside the neighbours who had lived next to them above ground and where thus able to exchange the terrible tidings of war as they had once exchanged gossip.

During the night, and sometimes in daylight when there was a lull in the bombing and shelling, they emerged from their burrows to scavenge for provisions and, headscarved and predatory, they didn't look much different from the days when they had shopped at the local *gastronom* or challenged the cashier's calculations on the abacus in *Univermag*. At least as they foraged in the rubble they didn't have to queue. But sometimes they didn't return and their old and their young were beckoned into another circle.

As Antonov and Razin followed Misha into the vaults of ground held by the Germans, occasionally surfacing to run from one haven to another, the numbers thinned out but those remaining had a permanent air about them and Misha explained that they were directly beneath the remains of their homes. 'Where someone died,' he added.

A women called out: 'Misha, come. Drink some soup.' She

wore black and was barrel-shaped and her eyes were small above the bunches of her cheeks, but for one surprising moment Antonov saw her as a young girl and her eyes were wide and clear as she peered into the future.

Misha whispered: 'She lost her two sons in the air-raid on August 23. I used to play with them, Georgi and Andrei. They were twins. People said they couldn't tell them apart but I could.'

The woman ladled soup into a wooden bowl. 'Here, drink, it's good stuff. I found some potatoes and cheese rind and some flour.' Steam rose from the bowl.

Misha looked at Antonov and Razin. 'Go on, drink it,' Razin told him.

Misha took the bowl from the woman. Arms crossed, she nodded with maternal approval as Misha put his lips to it.

Antonov looked around the cellar. An old man and woman sat close together inside a circle of battered possessions; outside the circle stood two heaps of small clothes and some wooden toys.

The woman turned to Antonov and Razin. 'What brings you down here?' she asked.

'Misha knows a tunnel where we can surprise some Fritzes.'

'Good. Kill as many parasites as you can. Soup?'

Antonov shook his head. 'We've just eaten.'

'Then you're lucky. But sit down and have a smoke.' She handed them a tin of *makhorka* and some newspaper. 'A drink?' She passed Antonov a bottle of vodka and when, smiling, he refused: 'You don't drink firewater? Are you sure you're a Russian soldier?'

'He's a Siberian,' Razin said, lighting an untidy cigarette, and Misha, leaning forward in the oily light of the stove, said: 'That's Yury Antonov,' but the name meant nothing to the woman and Antonov was relieved.

'Where in Siberia?' she asked.

'Near Novosibirsk.'

'Ah, I went to Tomsk once. A long time ago. And you?' to Razin.

'Kiev.'

90

But Kiev was beyond her horizons.

She said: 'I hear there are ice floes on the Volga.'

'Mushy stuff,' Antonov said. 'There will be ice on the Ob by now.'

'Ah,' she said, 'the Ob.'

'One of the longest rivers in the world.'

'The Volga's different,' dismissing the Ob. 'It takes a long time to freeze right over. But soon the ice-floes will be as hard as concrete and it will be very difficult to cross it. Any news of a counter-attack?' she asked Razin.

'There's always news of it but it never comes. If it does come this is how it will be.' Razin drew a diagram on the dust and the flagstones. 'From the south, fifty miles or so from Stalingrad, and from the north-west across the Don. That's where the Fritzes are weakest,' he explained.

'I've heard that re-inforcements are on the way,' the woman said.

'Let's hope the Fritzes haven't heard as well. If we do counter-attack and the armies from the north and south meet up then they will be surrounded in Stalingrad. Just as we are now. And you,' nodding at the woman and the old couple, 'will be able to escape across the Volga on an ice-floe.'

Misha began to hum *Katyusha*. Boris inched towards the food and warmth.

The woman said: 'Mother of God, that's the fattest rat I ever saw.'

'That's Boris,' Razin said.

The woman threw a stone at the rat; it retreated but not too far. 'Rats! They're making stews with them in some cellars.' She turned to Antonov. 'Do you have any brothers or sisters?'

'One, Alexander.'

'The same age as you?'

'Younger,' said Antonov, remembering that she had been the mother of twins.

'And you?' to Razin.

'Just me.'

'Enough, I shouldn't wonder. Rats! God in heaven. How old is Alexander?'

91

'Sixteen. He wants to be a pilot.'

'Didn't you?'

'I was medically unfit,' Antonov said. 'Then they found I could shoot straight.'

'Have you shot many Germans?'

'A few.'

'Shoot some more for me.' She poured vodka into a tin cup and drank it. 'Are your parents alive?' And when he said they were: 'Tell me about them.'

He told her about his mother's authority in the house, his father's affinity with the outdoors. He saw his mother masking the windows with newspaper to keep the cold at bay; saw his father hand-scything their own plot of wheat. He saw the frost patterns like ferns on the inside of his bedroom window; he breathed on them and his mother and father slithered away and he was back in the cellar.

'You like hunting?' the woman asked. 'Most Siberians do.'

'I went whenever I could.'

'So you like killing?'

'I never thought of it that way.'

'And now?'

'It has to be done.'

'That wasn't what I asked.'

'No,' he said, 'I don't like it,' and hoped he was telling the truth.

'I went hunting for food the other day,' she said. 'A soldier gave me a grenade. A pineapple, he called it. Like an egg with squares cut in it. He showed me how to use if it I was stopped by parasite soldiers. You pull out a pin and when you throw it the lever comes away from the egg and it explodes a few seconds later. Anyway I was stopped by a German soldier shouting at me from behind a wall. I had found some old cans of meat and I didn't want to lose them so, without really thinking, I pulled the pin and threw the pineapple and, because he was so surprised I suppose, the German didn't do anything about it and the pineapple exploded. His body was in a terrible state but his face . . . His face,' she repeated after a few moments, 'was very young. Perhaps nine years older

92

than . . . Anyway let's say nine years older than Misha.'

She looked at Misha but he was asleep on the flagstones. Gently she covered him with a blanket.

***

She woke them an hour before dawn. Shook them and gave them tea from an ancient samovar; the old couple slept on, arms round each other as if they were on their honeymoon.

'How do you feel?' she asked and when Antonov gave the old peasant reply: 'Better than tomorrow,' she smiled.

'How old are you?'

'Eighteen.'

'Quite a target with that fair hair of yours.'

'Don't worry,' he said, 'black hair's worse against snow.'

'God go with you.'

He felt her gaze lingering with them as Misha led the way through a trapdoor into what was left of her house. God go with you . . . in a society that had rejected religion.

He had mentioned these habitual references to God to Razin and the Ukrainian had replied: 'Communism is a religion.'

Misha said: 'We have to go above ground for a little way now.'

Outside the sleet had stopped but the night air had a snow-coldness about it, and the rubble was slippery underfoot as they made their way from the cellars of the State Brewery to the vaults of the State Bank to the basement of *Univermag*.

They were deep inside German-held territory.

Razin, pistol in hand, shone his flashlight. They were in the furniture depository; there was even a bed there; Razin lay on it and the springs played a few chords of rusty music.

He said to Misha: 'So where the hell are you taking us?'

'Beneath the stage of Gorki Theatre. Under Red Square to the railroad station. Through a tunnel to Tsaritsa Gorge. There's a church there overlooking my school.'

'So?'

'That's where Meister is.'

Razin, exploring the basement with the flashlight, said: 'Odd that Meister should have chosen your school.'

'It's a good hiding place.'

'A coincidence, though. Don't you think so?'

'I suppose so.' The flashlight lit Misha's face; his eyes were wide and dark in his sharp features.

'You took him there, didn't you? Got the watch for telling him where we were.'

'No!' Misha blinked; in the beam of the flashlight Antonov saw tears squeezed from beneath his eyelashes.

'Leave him alone,' Antonov said. 'There's no point.'

'Then came to us – and got a penknife.'

'I led you away from your tunnel.' Tears trickled down his cheeks.

'Who do you want to win Misha, Meister or Antonov?' Razin asked.

'Antonov, of course. I'm a Russian –'

'I know you do,' Antonov said. 'And I don't care how you got the watch and I *gave* you the knife. What does it matter? Soldiers go looting, the prizes of victory. And we're going to win, aren't we, Misha?'

Misha nodded, pressing his fingertips to his eyes.

'All right then, let's go to school, your school.'

***

The Katyusha exploded as they emerged from Gorki Theatre. It killed the big rat outright and knocked Antonov, Razin and the boy to the ground. The last thing Antonov saw before he lost consciousness were flakes of snow falling like feathers from the darkness above.

CHAPTER TWELVE

Antonov's mother came towards his bed, bedclothes smelling as always of warm cleanliness, carrying a bowl of steaming borsch. His father stood at the door, smoking rifle in his hands. Alexander stood on the bed-rail beating his chest like a gorilla.

A breeze coming from the wheatfields rippled the curtains and he could see cranes flying high in a summer sky. Tasya took the bowl from his mother and spooned borsch to him. When he refused it she offered her bare breast.

Then Alexander swung on a vine and Antonov caught his hand and Misha said: 'Not so hard, you're hurting,' and Razin, pulling on his moustache, said: 'Welcome back.'

To his left side it was very hot, to the right cold. He moved his left hand but Misha, hanging on, said: 'Don't, you'll burn yourself.'

He shut his eyes tight, opened them wide. The stove beside the stretcher was incandescent. He moved his right hand and touched wet earth studded with stones; like fruit in a cold plum pudding, he thought. He smelled hot metal and spent explosives. He heard growling voices.

He tried to raise himself on one elbow but his head was too heavy. It sounded as though there were an insect inside it. He turned so that he was staring at the grey sky. Razin's face came into view again, in duplicate.

Two mouths said: 'For God's sake don't say, "Where am

I?" I'll tell you. In a dug-out on the banks of the Volga near the Barricade factory. In a pocket 400 by 700 metres surrounded by Fritzes on one side and floating slush on the other.'

Antonov tried to ask what had happened but his tongue filled his mouth. A recurrent dream came back to him: he was standing on a platform trying to read a poem he had written but his lips were frozen.

A wave of Stukas flew overhead. He could feel the ground shaking with the wounds of battle.

Razin, face focussing into a single image, was speaking. '. . . owe everything to Misha. I misjudged him.'

Antonov tried to concentrate as Razin, corrected from time to time by Misha, told him what had happened after the Katyusha had exploded. But the words had wings and flew away.

He closed his eyes. Ah, better. The words returned and formed pictures. He saw himself lying beneath the hesitant snowflakes, saw Misha stand up, then Razin; heard them conversing in ragged whispers.

And they were dragging him into the ruin of Gorki Theatre, beneath the stage, Razin's flashlight picking out props – a harlequin costume, a carousel, a backdrop of a city sky-line.

Now Misha was running and he was looking down upon him as he navigated tunnels, trenches, cellars, sprinted through devastated streets, dodged German sentries shivering beneath snow-dusted helmets.

Once a sentry fired a shot and Misha fell, gashing his shin on a shard of broken glass. Antonov, eyes still closed, stretched out a hand and touched the boy's arm.

Razin's voice continued uninterrupted as Misha struggled to his feet and, keeping low, dodged between humps of masonry. The sentry fired again; Antonov cried out but no sound issued from his lips.

Finally Misha reached the thin Soviet lines stretched along the Volga. He was challenged by two sentries, gave the password and was escorted to a command-post where the duty officer for the night was a young lieutenant flexing his authority.

The lieutenant was at first reluctant to call Chuikov on the field telephone. But Misha could be both persuasive and threatening. He knew General Chuikov, he told the lieutenant. And the general would be very angry if the sniper pitted against Meister was allowed to die beneath the stage of the Gorki Theatre in German-held territory. And who in Moscow, Misha asked, voice breaking with effort, had instructed Chuikov to make sure that Antonov was given every assistance in his duel?

The lieutenant, knowing the answer, called Chuikov. Back came the answer: assemble a civilian storm group and bring back Antonov.

The lieutenant mustered a group, one of the units formed to infiltrate the German lines during darkness when the battleground wasn't laid bare to the enemy reconnaissance planes.

It consisted of an assault party armed with sub-machine-guns, grenades and spades sharpened for close fighting; a back-up group carrying mortars and explosives; a couple of snipers to give covering fire.

The storm group was commanded by an engineer named Gordov. His nose was flat, his eyes sunken and bloodshot, his brown beard embroidered with grey. Antonov, observing from above, sensed that the mission didn't appeal to him: his job was to kill Germans, not to save one pampered sniper.

Misha led the group back to Gorki Theatre where Antonov saw himself lying beneath the wrecked stage beside the carousel. It had stopped snowing and occasionally moonlight, finding windows in the clouds, shone through the floor-boards.

The back-up party, four of them, strapped him to a stretcher and set off towards the river while two scouts went ahead and two snipers brought up the rear.

They would have made it to the command post if a German patrol hadn't spotted them 100 metres the wrong side of the Russian lines. And they then might have been decimated if

97

the Germans, aware of the reputations of night assault parties, hadn't opened fire prematurely.

As it was the two scouts were hit and the stretcher-bearers were forced to veer away from the command post. Then the back-up gunners started shooting and the stretcher-bearers escaped.

'Misha will tell you why we're here,' Razin said. 'He knows about these things.'

'The Fritzes made another last-ditch attack,' Misha said. His voice had shrunk since Antonov last spoke to him, but it was still sharp with flints. 'They reached the river and cut us in two.'

'For the third time,' Razin said.

'We're with Lyudnikov's division to the east of the Barricade factory. He's only got 500 men left and his 650th Regiment is down to thirty-one men. To the north of the German bridgehead Gorokhov is holding out.'

'Just,' Razin said.

Antonov opened his lips and, like a man trying to conquer a stutter, attempted to mould words.

Razin held a tin mug to his lips. 'Here, this might help.' The water was cold and sweet. 'Sugar,' Razin explained. 'Part of our rations. Five grams of sugar and a couple of rusks. Very fortifying.'

Water dribbled down Antonov's chin. Was he paralysed? But some of the water oiled his tongue. When he spoke the words rolled out slowly like marbles. 'Last-ditch . . . Why last-ditch?'

Misha said: 'Because we're about to counter-attack to the north-west and south-east of Stalingrad. They say we've assembled over a million troops right under the noses of the Fritzes and their allies, Rumanians, Hungarians and Italians,' he explained. 'I heard that we've brought up 900 tanks and more than 1,000 aircraft,' he added casually.

'And here in Stalingrad?' The words came more easily and Antonov enjoyed them. 'How many troops?'

'Not many. Forty-thousand perhaps. Five hundred in this pocket. But we'll hold out until the counter-attack comes.'

Razin said: 'We're holding onto the west bank of the river by our bootlaces. And *when* the counter-attack comes we'll still be here encircled with the Germans.'

Another voice intruded, the deep voice of a man fortified by a beard. Antonov stared into the frame of grey sky and saw that Razin had been joined by a man who had to be Gordov. His face was pale and dirty but the black-and-grey beard looked freshly combed.

He perceived the beard as the man's pet and decided that the flesh beneath it was very soft.

Gordov said: 'Don't be so defeatist, comrade. When the attack comes the vermin will have to turn and meet it and the pressure will be off us. Then we'll get supplies, guns, ammunition.'

'How? Through the ice floes?'

'From the air. In any case the Volga will freeze soon.'

'From the air! Everything they've dropped so far has fallen into the river or into the German trenches.'

'You don't have much faith, comrade. What's your name?'

'Winston Churchill,' Razin said. 'What's it like holding a gun instead of a screwdriver?'

Old soldier versus civilian. But Antonov knew Razin was wrong to antagonise Gordov. Gordov had been invested with authority through battle: war had made him and he was brave with it. Lying there in the dug-out surrounded by battle Antonov knew many things.

He managed to turn and smile at Misha. Don't take any notice of them, the smile said. Misha smiled back.

Gordov combed his beard, his pet, with his fingers. 'What's it like being a wet-nurse? Why don't you nurse some of those poor bastards over the top?'

Misha explained to Antonov: 'There are 400 wounded lying beside the river. They've been there in the rain and snow and they can't get across to the other side because of the ice floes.'

'And because of an MG 34 mounted over there.' Gordov pointed. 'We've tried getting them across in row-boats but that bastard opens up and sinks them every time. But don't worry,' he said to Antonov, 'we'll do our best to get you across,' although he didn't sound enthusiastic.

'I don't want to go across,' Antonov said. 'I want to stay here.'

'Chuikov's orders,' Razin said. 'According to the medic you've got a suspected hairline fracture of the skull. You can't hunt Meister with a broken head.'

Razin had two faces again. A Stuka came in low, Jericho siren screaming. Its bombs fell close by, the earth shuddered, stones rattled into the dug-out.

Gordov said: 'Those fell among the wounded.'

A snowflake hesitated over the dug-out, dying as it got near the stove. Turning his head, Antonov noticed four or five other members of the assault group warming themselves round the glowing haunches of the stove. They wore *shapki* with the flaps pulled over their ears and knee-length boots and their faces were bleak with exhaustion. They were passing round a mug and smoking thin cigarettes rolled from newspaper. Occasionally one of them glanced dispassionately at Antonov. Razin joined them.

Misha, following Antonov's gaze, told him that the night before the rescue Gordov and his men, armed with pistols, knives and spades, feet muffled with sacking, had crept up to a German observation post, a wall of rubble in one corner of the devastated Red October Plant, and killed all the occupants in two minutes.

'Night is our time,' Misha said. The skin was tight across his cheekbones and his eyes, almost black, were deep in their sockets.

'And day is the German's time? Meister's time?'

'Day is your time too,' Misha said.

'We wouldn't have found Meister in the school, would we?'

'Maybe, maybe not. He might have been away looking for you.'

'We wouldn't have found him because you would have found a way of warning him. Why, Misha?'

Misha didn't answer for a moment. For one startling moment Antonov saw ancient wisdom in his eyes. Then he said: 'Because he's like you.'

And Antonov felt like confessing that he was glad he hadn't reached the school because he didn't want to kill Meister but he couldn't because boys must have heroes but he was glad he had confessed to himself.

But why don't I want to kill him? he asked himself. And then it occurred to him that not so long ago none of the millions of Germans and Russians engaged in combat had wanted to fight. That they set about killing each other simply because they were told to, taking lives without compassion because they were strangers to each other.

But not Meister and I. We know each other. If I kill Meister it will be a sort of suicide. But just supposing – and here Antonov began to suspect that he was feverish – that all the men fighting to the death over the lip of the dug-out *knew* each other. Would the fighting stop?

He patted Misha's hand. 'You and I know each other don't we, Alexander.'

'Who's Alexander?' Misha asked but Antonov didn't answer because his eyes were closed and there was a snow-smelling breeze reaching him from the black earth of the steppe and wolves were singing in the taiga and the lighted windows of the wooden cottage were beckoning him home.

***

Antonov surfaced again at dusk as they discussed the plan to knock out the German machine-gunner dominating this stretch of the Volga.

He distinguished Gordov's bearded voice. 'We've got a couple of men from Lyudnikov's 179th Engineers to finish the tunnel. That should take three hours. We hit the vermin at 2200 hours. Any questions?'

No one questioned him, this leader re-fashioned by circumstances. 'Don't use guns if you can help it, we're down to twenty rounds per person. Don't worry about grenades – we haven't got any left.'

How were they going to kill the machine-gunners? With sharpened spades? With their bare hands?

Antonov looked for Misha; he was asleep under a filthy blanket. He could see slits of darkening sky between planks placed over the dug-out to hide the glow of the stove from the Germans. He heard German bombers returning to base leaving the sky free. He felt frost nosing down the sides of the dug-out; in Siberia the permafrost stayed a few metres below the surface forever.

'After they've fixed the MG 34,' Razin said to Antonov, 'we will be taken across the river in a row-boat.'

'And have beds, and plump nurses to keep you warm,' Gordov said, towering over the stretcher. 'But don't think we're knocking out the machine-gun just for your sake: we want to get the wounded over to the east bank as well.'

In the lull after the day's fighting Antonov could hear them sighing.

'You must take them before me,' Antonov said.

'You're more important,' Gordov said without meaning it. 'Chuikov says so. Moscow says so.'

Razin said to Gordov: 'Why are you in charge? Why not the military?'

'Because we know Tsarytsin. Its tunnels and its cellars, its secret places. Because it's our city. Because we care.'

'And we don't?'

'You might care about the Soviet Union, not about Tsarytsin. The old name for Stalingrad,' he explained. 'Derived from the Tartar words for yellow sand. It was built to protect the Russians from what was left of the Golden Horde. And it has been fought over many times. In the Civil War the Reds defended it against the Whites.'

'So you're a historian as well as an engineer?'

'Should I be ashamed?' Gordov stroked his beard. 'Are you anything else but a soldier?'

Antonov said: 'If you're not going to use guns or grenades what are you going to use?'

'You'll see.' Gordov produced a silver watch from inside his patched sheepskin jacket. 'Five minutes. They're putting up a diversionary barrage from the other side of the river. That usually means supplies are being rowed across. The Fritz machine-gunners will be looking for the row-boats, not us.'

The assault party were silhouettes behind the stove. One by one they disappeared. When Antonov looked round Misha was gone too.

***

'They burned them,' Misha said later.

'With a flame-thrower,' Gordov explained.

'They were covered in flames,' Misha said. 'They rolled on the ground trying to put them out.'

'They had killed many Russians,' Gordov said.

'They were burned alive.'

Misha's eyes stared at Antonov in the light from the stove. His face was masked with wildness.

'You shouldn't have been there,' Gordov said.

'Roasted alive,' Misha said. 'They were screaming. Calling to God.'

'It was the only way,' Gordov said. 'We had no grenades. We couldn't have started a shooting match. Not against a machine-gun.'

The bottom half of the mask that was Misha's face trembled.

Antonov said: 'Don't be ashamed of crying. Don't ever be that. Don't ever try and be tough.'

And when Misha began to cry he said: 'That's it, that's real bravery,' and stretched out his hand to the boy.

***

The row-boat slid onto the sandy mud at 2315 hours as a flare lit the river finding grey corpuscles of ice and slush in its dark blood.

German mortars and machine-guns opened up, firing at anything that moved, even ice-floes. But there were no splashes in the water opposite the dug-out.

Antonov, lying on the stretcher beside the small waves, shaded his eyes against the brightness of the flare. The river-smell was strong in his nostrils and the buzzing filled his head again.

Kneeling beside him in the mud, Razin said: 'We're taking off as soon as the flare has gone out.'

'You're not staying here?'

'You forget, I've got to protect you. And those plump nurses Comrade Gordov was talking about.'

The flare began to fade.

Gordov came up behind them, mud sucking at his boots. 'We can't waste this boat,' he said. 'There are six others coming with you.'

Razin said: '*We* can't? Who's we?'

'Lyudnikov. If you stay here there's room for one more casualty.'

'Orders are orders,' Razin said. 'And you know where mine come from.'

'Not heaven,' Gordov said and Antonov asked: 'Can we take the boy?'

'He doesn't want to go. In any case he's valuable to us.'

Antonov noticed Misha standing behind Gordov. 'No?'

Misha shook his head. 'I'm needed here.' He sounded very important.

The flare spent itself. Razin lifted Antonov from the stretcher and laid him in the bottom of the row-boat. Razin and the wounded sat on the bench-seats propping each other up.

Gordov, a silhouette again, pushed the boat with his boot.

Antonov, leaning on one elbow, waved and as the first ice floe ground against the hull, the lesser of the two silhouettes waved back.

CHAPTER THIRTEEN

Meister, cleaning his rifle beneath the two shrivelled fruit adorning the fingers of the pear tree in the school playground, considered Mankind.

No man is an Island . . . He had once believed Donne as he had believed everything he had been taught. No longer. Now he questioned.

Countries, cities, villages, men and women – islands, all of them. A man only interprets through his own perception therefore he is self-contained.

But, gazing down the barrel of the Karabiner, Meister conceded that we are floating islands drifting occasionally into each other's lives. Destiny? Too grand. It was circumstance that navigated those islands; circumstance that introduced husband to wife; circumstance that propelled a young German from Hamburg into conflict with a young Russian from Siberia.

What else could it be? I learned to shoot because, family wealth apart, I had nothing to offer; Antonov learned to shoot because his father was a hunter. Hitler and Stalin went to war and became our patrons and we were matched and that wasn't destiny, it was circumstance.

And now, islands that have barely touched, we are drifting apart. He sensed it and was surprised at the eddies of emotion. Regret and relief. We didn't know each other but we knew each other well.

'You look as if you've lost a mark and found a pfennig.' Lanz handed Meister a mug of coffee. 'Don't let the date get you down.'

It was Friday, November 13. Two days earlier Paulus had launched a frenzied attack on the factories to the north of Stalingrad, Red October and Barricade in particular, splitting the remnants of the Soviet forces. But everyone knew that the attack had faltered; that the 6th Army was a bloodied bull, head bowed in bewilderment. Everyone, that was, except strategists in faraway places.

Lanz said: 'It looks as if Antonov has laid down his arms even if Chuikov hasn't.' He thrashed his arms against his sides; the Russians' ally, the cold, was on the rampage and their bodies ached before its assault.

Lanz took a cigarette from a green packet and lit it, inhaled like a man struggling to stay alive, and coughed ferociously.

'That's all a sniper needs,' Meister said, 'someone beside him coughing like a machine-gun.' He leaned his rifle against the pear tree and wrapped a scarf under his chin and over his head to protect his ears; Lanz wore a Russian *shapka* with ear-flaps; he had offered one to Meister but Meister didn't want to wear dead men's clothes.

Lanz threw more schoolbooks onto the small fire he had built, a cadet version of *Das Kapital* among them. According to the wall clock on the floor it was lunchtime but the clock was two hours fast.

Lanz, cigarette in one hand, mug of coffee in the other, said: 'You needn't bother about me coughing. We won't be together much longer: the bird has flown. If Antonov was still in Stalingrad he would have found us here because this is where that little bastard Misha would have brought him. Where else? He finds us a nice quiet hideout, dumps us and fetches Antonov to finish us off.'

'No.' Meister shook his head emphatically. 'Antonov hasn't flown. Something's happened.'

After leaving the tunnel they had returned to the school to wait, convinced that Antonov was on his way. That, while Lanz kept watch, Meister could pick him off because Misha

106

was right, the school was a good vantage point. But that was three days ago and there had been no sign of Antonov.

'What do you mean, *something's happened*?'

'Maybe he got hurt.'

'You feel his wounds?'

'I think something's happened, that's all. Look at it logically. The Russians wouldn't pull him out: they still want him to kill me: they still want victory.'

Meister stood on a pile of rubble and peered over the wall. Before the battle there couldn't have been much of a view but now you could see the river in the distance; the shells and bombs had seen to that. When they came to rebuild Stalingrad they wouldn't need foundations: its bedrock was steel. He focussed his field-glasses. Snow hadn't settled yet but on the river he could see packs of slush and ice jostling each other. If Antonov had been wounded he would have been taken across the Volga, through the stampeding ice. The emotion Meister felt was disconcerting, a parting of flesh.

Lanz threw an atlas on the fire, burning the world. 'Aren't you glad he's gone?'

'In a way.'

'You didn't want to kill him, did you?'

'But I would have.'

'And you would have condemned yourself as a murderer?'

'I don't think,' Meister said, using words as stepping stones to some great truth, 'that anyone really wants to kill anyone else. But in war rules are laid down. Killing rules. Antonov and I broke the rules. We identified each other.' The stepping stones petered out.

'But you don't mind killing other Russians?'

'I don't want to but it's in the book of rules.'

'Who wrote the book?'

'A minority. That's all I know. A minority single-minded enough to control a majority who merely want to live in peace.'

A child's history of the Civil War followed the atlas into the flames.

'It all seemed so simple before I left Germany,' Meister

said. 'The Bolshevik menace had to be destroyed.' He gestured at the flattened city. 'Look at the Bolshevik menace now.' The sound of battle continued to reach them from the north.

'If they fight the way they're fighting at the factories the Bolsheviks could conquer the world,' Lanz said. 'They're fighting with their balls in the river and still they won't give up. And soon they'll counter-attack and you know something? We'll be cut off but we won't have a river to escape across.'

A motor-cyclist in field grey drove down the road, ruts of mud frozen into iron ridges, and stopped outside the school. Pushing his goggles onto his forehead, he unstrapped a tin canister and handed it to them. 'Rabbit stew,' he said.

'Pussycat,' Lanz said.

'And bread and cheese.'

'Soap,' Lanz said.

'Don't eat it then,' the motor-cyclist said. 'I will.' He was young and blond and dusty with wide, slanting eyes. He was attached to the 336th Sapper Battalion which explained his cockiness; they had just flown from Magdeburg to support the November 11 attack and he hadn't grown old with Stalingrad.

He leaned against the wall. 'Well,' he said making a performance of lighting a cigarette, 'it won't be long now.'

Lanz inspected his stew. 'It just meowed,' he said.

'What won't be long?' Meister asked.

'Victory,' the motor-cyclist said. 'Look what we brought from Germany.' He fished in the pocket of his tunic, produced a folded poster and opened it up. Black letters proclaimed THE FALL OF STALINGRAD. 'We've got thousands of them and we'll make the Ivans eat them,' he said replacing the poster in his pocket carefully, as though it were a banknote.

'Taste better than this stew,' Lanz said.

'I told you, I'll eat it.'

'You eat your poster.'

'That reminds me of a joke. I was taking my dog for a walk when I was a kid and a man stopped me and said, "Does your

108

dog bite?" And when I said, "No," he said, "Then how does it eat its dinner?"' The motor-cyclist laughed displaying very white, uneven teeth. When he had finished laughing he said: 'So you're Meister.'

'He's Meister,' Lanz said.

'I read about you in Magdeburg,' the motor-cyclist said. 'I never thought I'd meet you. It's an honour.'

'You shouldn't believe everything you read,' Meister told him.

'Where's Antonov? Around here?' The motor-cyclist looked eagerly around.'

'We don't know.'

'You mean he's run away?'

'No,' Meister said, 'I don't mean that.'

'Well, you haven't much more time. As soon as we push the Ivans into the river that will be the end of your duel.'

'They're taking some pushing,' Lanz said, spooning stew into his mouth.

'Is that your rifle?' the motor-cyclist asked, reaching for the Karabiner but dropping his hand when Meister snapped: 'Don't touch it.'

Meister said: 'Where are you from?'

'Munich. I've seen the Führer there a couple of times. What does it take to make a sniper?'

'You have to discriminate,' Meister said.

'Ah.' The motor-cyclist looked puzzled. And then: 'I envy you. You know, the sense of satisfaction. You're actually killing Russians instead of merely driving a motor-cycle. But still, I suppose I am doing a worthwhile job. You know, keeping Karl Meister supplied with food so that he can shoot Antonov on a full stomach. When I write home I'll tell them I supplied Karl Meister with rabbit stew.'

'Cat stew,' Lanz said, placing a piece of pale cheese onto a hunk of bread and popping it into his mouth with a furtive movement as though it were stolen.

Meister handed his canister to the motor-cyclist. 'You eat this, I'm not hungry.'

The motor-cyclist dipped a spoon into the stew. With the

109

spoon halfway to his mouth he turned to Lanz. 'You were joking, weren't you? You know, about cats . . .' Without waiting for a reply he put down the spoon.

Before leaving he asked Meister for his autograph. 'You know, for the people back home.' Meister scrawled it on the back of the FALL OF STALINGRAD.

Bug-eyed again with his goggles in place, the motor-cyclist kick-started his machine and, waving, took off down the frozen track.

The shell exploded so near to the school that it showered Meister and Lanz with debris. When Meister peered over the wall all he could see of the motor-cycle was one wheel spinning beside the shell-hole, the grave.

Skipping away in the breeze, heading for the river, was the poster; as it unfolded it reminded Meister of a fledgling bird, spreading its wings for the first time but looking just the same for its nest.

**

At 9.00 that evening Lanz heard a noise above the rattle of gunfire and the whine of an iced wind nosing through the jagged walls of the school.

He touched Meister's arm, put his finger to his lips, a thief hearing a footstep on gravel, the creak of a door opening.

They had decided to wait until dawn before reporting to Paulus that, in their opinion, Antonov was no longer in Stalingrad. They had moved the burning schoolbooks to the grate in the ruins of the classroom and, wrapped in blankets, were watching knowledge go up in flames, sparks racing up the sawn-off chimney to return through the open roof like words trying to make sense again.

Meister listened. He couldn't hear anything except the normal sounds of nocturnal Stalingrad. Lanz picked up his pistol and left the classroom. Meister saw him, dark and feline, scale the wall in the playground, drop to the other side on sponge feet. Meister picked up his rifle and, through a shell-hole, thrust the barrel into the night.

Finger hooked on the trigger, shoulder muscles tensed, he waited. Only when he had a target in the sights could he relax, stroke the trigger, breath gently. An aircraft lumbered overhead; a searchlight switched the sky; tracer bullets glowed and died.

Supposing he shot Lanz?

He had allowed Elzbeth to fire his rifle once on the banks of the Elbe. In fact he had done everything except pull the trigger, standing behind her, easing the butt into her shoulder, aiming the sights at a pine tree and feeling her warmth through her silk blouse.

The row startled him. Shouting, scuffling, cursing on the other side of the school. He ran to the space where the door had been as Lanz led in Misha squirming.

Lanz pushed him onto the blankets in front of the fire. 'Antonov hasn't quit,' Lanz said. 'That little bastard was leading him here.'

'Were you?' Meister asked in Russian. 'Were you leading Antonov here?'

'I was trying to save you,' Misha shouted. He tried to get up but Lanz pinned him with his boot.

'I don't know what he said,' Lanz said. 'But whatever it was I don't believe it.'

Meister said: 'What do you mean, trying to save us?'

Misha told him that Antonov had been wounded and taken to a hospital on the other side of the river.

'Badly wounded?'

'I don't know. He looked at me in a funny sort of way and kept wiping his forehead as though he was trying to get rid of something. But that's not the point, not now. You're in danger . . . ' He tried to get up again but Lanz's boot went for his throat.

When Meister translated Lanz said: 'Ask him where Antonov was injured,' and when Meister had translated the answer Lanz said: 'My local geography isn't too good but isn't that on the way here from the tunnel?'

When Misha agreed Lanz said with a sort of negative triumph: 'You see, he *was* leading Antonov here. Then they

111

got shot up. Maybe Antonov was concussed, who knows. But if you think he's on the other side of the river you're crazy. He's here. Outside. Looking for you.'

Meister said to Misha: 'Is Antonov here?'

'I told you, he's on the other side of the Volga.' He blinked. 'If he made it.'

Misha said that an assault group had been sent to rescue Antonov, that a row-boat from Vice-Admiral Rogachev's Volga Flotilla had set off across the river with him on board.

'But how are we in danger?' Meister asked.

Misha said: 'I knew two members of the assault group before the Germans came. They lived near the bakery. They were bad men and they robbed my father once. I heard them talking the day after Antonov left. They were talking about killing you.'

Misha paused and Meister thought: He should be in bed dreaming about football, not talking about killing.

'What's he saying?' Lanz asked but Meister held up his hand. 'Why do they want to kill me?' he asked Misha.

'They think they will become heroes. Get medals. Good jobs when the war is over.'

'Then they're stupid. If I'm going to be killed Antonov's got to do the job. They won't get medals, they'll get bullets.'

'They asked me to lead them to you but I refused. Look.' Meister noticed the swellings on his face, dried blood at the corner of his mouth. 'I ran away but they'll still find you. Razin told them where you were. There was no reason why he shouldn't.'

'Razin?'

Lanz, picking out the one word, said: 'Me, Russian version.'

'They're stupid all right,' Misha said, 'but they're dangerous and they might be outside now waiting for you to show yourself.'

'Then I won't.' Meister gave him coffee and a slab of bitter chocolate. 'You stay here, don't move, right?'

Misha said: 'Right.'

When Meister translated what Misha had told him Lanz

said: 'I don't believe him.'

'You think everyone's lying.'

'Wrong. But I do think Antonov's out there.'

'It doesn't matter, does it? Antonov or two bounty hunters, they're all trying to kill us.'

'It matters to you,' Lanz said.

'Maybe. It also matters to me that I stay alive.' Meister picked up his rifle. 'I'll take the front because that's the way they'll come, up from the river. You take the back in case I'm wrong. We'll wait until they think we're asleep. Then they'll show themselves because they're stupid.

'Antonov isn't,' Lanz said.

'Antonov isn't out there.'

'Supposing they've got grenades?'

Meister asked Misha if they had grenades.

'No pineapples,' Misha said. 'Lyudnikov's hardly got any bullets let alone grenades.' He opened his eyes wide, fighting sleep.

Meister positioned himself beside a shell-hole; to his right he could see Misha in front of the fire; he could tell from the curl of his body that he was asleep.

The wind had dropped and the clouds had parted in places and from time to time the moon shone through the rents; Meister hoped the two Russians would come when the moon was shining.

Time passed neither swiftly nor slowly; it had no dimension when Meister was waiting. Born in another place, he reflected, he might have been a hunter like Antonov. Circumstance.

He didn't mind the waiting because in a way it didn't exist: his senses melded. Familiarity with the gun, the occasional cough of combat as Russian marauders went about their work, a taste of rust, the moon projecting lonely pictures, the cold night in his nostrils.

He enjoyed the smell of night in Stalingrad, its misty flavour of gestation, because it was normality which by day was thrust aside by shells and bombs. When danger was close he sometimes smelled perfume.

113

He returned to Hamburg but his gaze didn't waver from the rubble, now black, now silver. When he had decided to become a sharp-shooter he had been taken with a dozen other aspirants to a shooting range adjoining Landungsbrücken railway station by the harbour.

A brisk middle-aged instructor wearing civilian clothes as though they were a uniform, who was said to have been a sniper in the 1914–18 war, made them lie in a row on coconut mats. As he kicked their legs into position he said: 'This is just to see if you've got the makings of a marksman. If not you can go home and take up knitting.' His voice in the cordite-smelling, barn-like range reminded Meister of biscuits breaking.

They were given .22 training rifles almost identical to the Mauser 98a but manufactured for use with small-calibre ammunition to comply with the Treaty of Versailles, and told to fire six rounds at conventional black and white targets.

When Meister wound back his target there wasn't a mark on it but his neighbour's target was drilled with twelve bullet holes.

But the instructor wasn't as snappy as he sounded. Kneeling beside Meister whose face was pressed into his mat, he said: 'Don't worry, son, it happened to me once. Stay behind after the others have gone.' And to Meister's neighbour: 'One word about this and I'll kick your backside from here to Berlin.'

Later Meister peppered the bull and magpie with bullets and the instructor said: 'You're going to be good, son, really good and I wish I was going with you wherever that is.'

Kneeling beside the shell-hole, Meister experienced again the despair he had felt when, gazing at his blank target, he had believed that he would never command respect in Magdalena's set and even now felt hot with shame although, since Stalingrad, he knew that it had never mattered anyway.

Glancing at Misha, curled like a foetus, he wished that he had found out earlier in his life that such values are smoke screening truth.

He squeezed the trigger gently as a shape that hadn't been

114

in his vision before moved in the moonlight. Stupid but then they were stupid. He squeezed the trigger harder and the shape reared and fell forward.

He waited. *Two* members of an assault group.

Misha joined him. Meister didn't look down. He stroked the trigger, light, downward movements. He doubted whether he would have to shoot again but it was important to keep contact with the gun.

'. . . *really good and I wish I was going with you wherever that is.*' The instructor had died just before Britain declared war in 1939; a fragment of shrapnel that had been pressing on an artery since 1917.

The gunshot didn't startle him. Nor the scream. But he relaxed his hold on the Karabiner and his finger forgot the trigger.

Lanz said: 'All right, I was wrong: it wasn't Antonov. And yes, they were stupid, weren't they. Stupid and dead.'

When Meister told Misha what had happened he went back to the fire frowning. He sat for a while staring into the glowing remains of knowledge.

Lanz said to him: 'It wasn't true, was it, what you told us about your father?'

'No,' Misha said. 'Both my mother and father were killed in the Stalingrad during the fighting,' and he burrowed deep into the blankets.

***

At dawn, as the big guns broke open the day, Meister asked Misha: 'Why did you do it? Why did you warn us? Don't you know we're the enemy?'

And Misha said: 'You're not the enemy. And Antonov isn't your enemy.'

'Then who is?' Meister asked but Misha merely threw another schoolbook onto the rekindled fire and watched the sparks chase each other up the chopped-off chimney.

***

115

The following morning, after he had stolen breakfast, Lanz made a football. He constructed it with book-binding, sacking and an old pair of shoes and bound it with string and it was almost spherical.

'How did you play with only one goal?' he asked Misha, pointing at the posts chalked on the wall.

'We had two teams', Misha told him. 'And we just kicked it about and tried to score goals and whoever happened to be in goal was allowed to use his hands to stop it.'

'Then that's how we'll play it,' Lanz said. 'You and me. Five minutes each half. Russia versus Germany. I'll kick off – just as we did last year.'

At half-time, timed by Meister on the school clock, the score was 1–1. Misha, pale face polished pink by cold and exertion, still looked fit but Lanz, breath steaming like a race-horse's after a gallop, had to lean against the wall.

In the second half he recovered, racing around the playground on his bow legs, teaching Misha a trick or two with the ball. One minute from the end he scored.

'Come on Russia,' Meister called out.

He looked at the clock. Thirty seconds to go. But Lanz's legs were bending. He attempted some fancy footwork; Misha took the ball from him. As Misha steadied himself to shoot Lanz ran back to the goal.

Misha shot. Lanz got his fingers to the ball but it hit the wall inside the posts.

'Full-time,' Meister shouted.

'But nobody won,' Misha said.

'Nobody every does,' Lanz said.

CHAPTER FOURTEEN

The ice-floes were trying to shoulder the row-boat out of their river. Or send it to the bottom. The shudders as they ground against the hull passed through Antonov's body.

Unable to see the water from the bottom of the boat – just the dark sky and the heaving arms of the oarsmen – he imagined them as sharks on the attack.

Razin's voice reached him from the huddle of wounded soldiers. 'We're half way across.'

A yellow flare lit the sky. Antonov shut his eyes but its brilliance penetrated his eyelids.

Soviet guns on the east bank fired a few salvoes and German machine-gunners raked the river but the bullets were a long way from the row-boat: the flame-thrower had seen to that.

When the flare died the cold advanced up his leg. He saw his father, brown face half-mooned with white by the peak of the cap he wore in the fields, paddling in the clear waters of the Ob, trousers rolled up to his knees, giving him swimming lessons.

From the river beach, his mother, pregnant with Alexander, transmitted smiles of encouragement. She set great store by swimming, regarding it as a sophisticated accomplishment practised outside their land-locked steppe and today he was expected to conquer the breast-stroke.

But the water this June day in the Silver Birch Festival was icy and his father had as much idea of swimming as he had of ballet-dancing. 'Go on,' he said, 'in you go. Kick with your legs, push the water aside with your arms.' He made vague thrusting motions with his hands as though he were pushing aside undergrowth in the taiga.

In fact he wasn't interested in whether his son could swim or not – water was for fish – but at festival time he indulged his wife, rewarding her for the years of toil. Today he had bought her a pair of miniature birch-bark shoes.

Yury, not hearing authority in his father's voice, stayed in the shallows, white and stiff and pimpled with cold, while his mother, plump face bunched with frustration, gestured from the beach.

Behind the beach couples played ping-pong on sagging tables; on the grey sand families spread themselves in the sun; in the water young men wearing bathing costumes that, when saturated, drooped alarmingly at the crotch, chased girls and splashed them.

'Go on,' his father urged. 'For your mother's sake.'

'I'll sink,' Yury protested.

His father pointed at the young men and girls. 'They aren't sinking.'

'They were taught to swim.'

'I'm teaching you.'

Yury thought his father should be standing in the water, gun in hand, waiting for duck to fly into his vision.

From the beach he heard his mother's pleading voice. And heard her in the future, beside the water pump: 'Of course Yury can swim now.' She had never attached much importance to shooting.

His father said: 'If I had a swimming costume I'd join you.' He smiled to show that it was a joke; adults often did that. 'Come on, for your mother's sake,' wanting to get it over with, sink or swim.

Yury stared at the clear water. Tresses of weed moved lazily. He took a step forward and mud spiralled to the surface. A tiny fish, contemplating the disturbance, darted away.

118

Tensing his muscles, drawing a deep breath, he threw himself forward . . .

The cold advanced rapidly, almost covering his legs. He shouted: 'Hey, we're filling up with water,' remembering that, on that sunlit, silver-birch day, he hadn't swum a single stroke and never had since.

Razin reached down. 'Shit, it's pouring in,' he called out.

'Then block it,' one of the oarsmen called out.

Another ice-floe hit the boat, then another. The sharks, Antonov thought, had smelled a wounded prey. He saw their teeth on the other side of the hull.

'Christ it's cold,' Razin shouted.

The water reached Antonov's hip: soon only his head would be clear, if he could raise it.

Razin called out: 'Bale you stupid bastards, bale.'

Antonov saw a steel helmet scoop water from beside him. The water was in his ears drowning sound. He raised his head, sound returned. But he couldn't hold up his head for more than a few seconds. He heard Razin shout: 'I can't feel my hand: my arm's like a stump.'

The steel helmet dipped and scooped.

'How much further?' Antonov asked.

'Farther than that,' Razin said and his voice sounded frozen too.

The back of Antonov's neck ached from supporting his head; any moment now he would have to lay it back gently and let the water into his ears, into his nostrils and down to his lungs. A stupid way to drown, lying on the bottom of a row-boat. He trembled with the cold and the proximity of the unknown.

He eased his head into the water. Shut his eyes as he waited for it to extinguish hearing and breathing. The water reached the lobes of his ears, stopped.

Razin said: 'I can't feel my arm.'

The oarsmen grunted as they pulled. The steel helmet filled and emptied, then paused. The water rose above the lobes of Antonov's ears. He tried to raise his head again but it was too heavy.

He felt the nose of a big ice-shark butt the hull. *Saw* it wheel and return. The boat shuddered.

Antonov heard Razin cry out. The cry submerged. The water was ice in his nostrils but gentle on his eyes. He breathed a little water. He cried out a bubble of sound. He tried to swim but he had no faith and, apologising to his mother on the beach, he floundered between his father's legs, a deathly white beneath the rolled-up trousers.

***

Snow fell on November 16 and settled in for winter.

Its luminosity was the first thing Antonov noticed when he regained consciousness. He saw the whiteness through a window of the hospital and he knew that outside it was beautiful.

There had been periods of awareness before but this was the first true awakening. He wanted to feel snow polished underfoot on a wooden track and he wanted to skate on a yard that had been hosed into a rink.

He turned his head and saw Razin in a moulting blue dressing-gown sitting beside the bed, one arm in a sling, reading the chart that should have been hanging on the end of his bed.

Razin said: 'You nearly drowned.' He tapped the chart. 'But you're on the mend. Stout peasant stock.'

'Siberian stock,' Antonov said. 'What about the others?'

'Two died – they hadn't got enough limbs to swim with. But they were going to die anyway.'

Flakes of snow hesitated at the window.

'Did I swim?' Antonov asked incredulously.

'Like a stone. But we were near the shore and the water wasn't deep and one of the oarsmen got you ashore. The others managed to swim.'

'And you?' Somehow Antonov couldn't imagine Razin swimming.

'I thought of those plump nurses: I made it.'

'How's your arm?'

'Thawing.' With his good hand Razin held the arm in the sling as though it belonged to a stranger. 'Exposure, not quite the same as frostbite, according to the medics. And rare in just one limb. They're very interested in me, those boys. They want to see if it turns gangrenous and starts to spread. If it does, chop.' He aimed the blade of his good hand at the sling.

Razin's face became fuzzy. Antonov shut his eyes. When he opened them Razin had two faces once again.

'What's the matter?' Razin asked.

'There are two of you.'

'They were afraid of that, double vision. They got all the water out of your lungs but they weren't as worried about those as they were about your sight.'

'Scared I won't be able to shoot Meister?'

'Double vision isn't exactly an asset for a sniper. Especially when a hair-line fracture of the skull has been confirmed,' he added. He settled himself comfortably in the chair. 'Let's hope your vision stays that way until the war's over.'

Leaning his head, shaved and bandaged, on the stacked pillows, Antonov looked around. The bed was surrounded by screens; beyond them he could hear desultory talk and the sighs of men in pain.

He asked Razin if Moscow still wanted him to kill Meister.

'Why not? Nothing's changed. You still humanise statistics. There are so many dead, so many wounded, that figures lose their impact. But you're every mother's son.'

So is Meister, Antonov thought.

'If you kill Meister they'll toast you in every home in the Soviet Union. Sergei, Stepan, Mikhail, Nikolai . . . They're alive and well and beating the hell out of the Fritzes.'

'Maybe it won't come to that.' Razin's two faces became one again. Through the window Antonov could see the white church with the green dome.

'The counter-attack? That won't make any difference. When it comes, if it comes, you and Meister will still be in Stalingrad. But not,' Razin added thoughtfully, 'if you're still over here on the east bank. How long do you think you can drag it out?'

121

'Until I'm cured.'

'You can do better than that.'

'I can't fake a fractured skull.'

'You can fake double-vision. Nothing simpler. Why not try triple-vision?'

'You don't have to go back,' Antonov said. 'Not if your hand's still bad.'

'Wrong. Wherever you go I go. You're my meal ticket. If you cross the river without me then they'll stick me in the front-line again.'

Antonov said: 'Strange, isn't it, a river separating us from hell.' Razin's face was slipping out of focus again.

'The Dneiper is a more impressive river,' Razin said. 'A monarch. On summer evenings we used to stroll along its banks and if you had a girl on your arm you bought her a carnation with a stem wrapped in silver paper.' Razin stared into the past. 'Did you know that Christianity was introduced into Russia via the Dneiper in the tenth century when Prince Vladimir ordered his subjects to be baptised in its waters? And did you know that there's a Golden Gate like Constantinople's in Kiev and a monastery built inside caves?'

Antonov shook his head cautiously but the movement disturbed an ache in his skull.

'You should learn some Ukrainian,' Razin told him. '"Ya ne razoomayoo" and "Do pobáchenya." "I don't understand" and "Goodbye."'

'Do pobáchenya,' Antonov said and slept.

***

The Russian counter-attack, code-named Uranus, was launched on November 19, a Thursday, about 100 miles north-west of Stalingrad. But Antonov didn't hear details until four days later.

They were brought to him by Razin, wearing the same dressing-gown and trading conspiratorial smiles with a nurse with Mongol features and shiny blue-black hair cut in a fringe.

The offensive, he told Antonov, began at 7.30 am in

freezing fog. An eighty-minute bombardment by Katyushas, heavy guns and mortars.

At 8.50 assault troops and tanks attacked in the snow-covered steppe south of the Don.

Razin recited units involved – 47th Guards, 5th Tank, 124th Rifle Division . . . But they meant nothing to Antonov; he saw snow, churned brown and blood-red, littered with the bodies of men who had met for the first time.

Razin said: 'They were fighting Rumanians mostly, the Third Army. The Rumanians fought well but what could they do with 100 old Czech light tanks against T-34s? By midday they were on the run.'

He took a packet of *papirosy* from the pocket of the dressing gown. 'Can I?' He folded a smile at the nurse.

'You shouldn't. Rules . . . '

'Made to be broken.' He lit the yellow cigarette.

So Razin had made a conquest. What did the girl see in him? A way with words, perhaps, that would be uncommon among her other patients; the mystery of his squandered intelligence; a cavalier attitude to authority . . . The girl, Antonov felt, wanted to know the source of every wandering line on Razin's face.

'Elsewhere,' Razin said, 'we didn't have such an easy time of it. We ran into Paulus's left flank and the Panzers fought like bastards. But we continued to advance towards Kalach. Here look.'

Razin produced a sketch-map. Kalach was about fifty miles west of Stalingrad. The idea, he explained, was for the Russians advancing from the north west to link up there with a force attacking from the south-east sealing Paulus's Sixth Army in a pocket.

Razin went on: 'The attack from the south-east was launched on the 20th. We ripped into the Rumanians all right. They fought well but their worst enemy was the steppe. A white wilderness. Even some of our brigade commanders lost their sense of direction and charged straight into enemy minefields.'

'So, what's happening now?' the nurse asked, proud of

Razin's expertise.

'Patience.' Razin sucked smoke into his lungs. 'Wait till you hear this. As you know the Don makes a sharp turn and flows south so, to reach Kalach, our forces advancing from the north-west had to cross it. And cross it they did with German tanks leading them.'

'I don't understand,' Antonov said.

'We drove five captured tanks over the bridge at night-time with their lights on the way the Germans drive them. Half way across the tanks stopped and out swarmed sixty Russians armed with sub-machine-guns. The Fritzes were caught with their pants down and the infantry swarmed over the bridge.'

Antonov had never seen Razin so animated. He wasn't sure what was responsible – the presence of the girl, the Russian victories or the fact that he was remote from them.

'And?' the girl asked impatiently.

Razin nipped his cigarette in the wash-basin and returned the butt to the packet. Then, settling himself once more, he announced: 'At 1030 hours today our forces linked up at Sovetski south-east of Kalach. The German Sixth Army, comrades, is surrounded.'

The girl purred. Razin looked as though he had done the job himself He said: 'Now Paulus will have to turn his guns the other way.'

'Just in time,' Antonov said. 'We were almost in the river.'

'*We* were in the river,' Razin reminded him.

The nurse said: 'Is your arm hurting you?' which Antonov thought was wonderful because she was supposed to be looking after him.

'It's not too bad.' Razin patted his bad arm with his good hand.

'Will it be over soon?' she asked. 'Stalingrad, I mean.'

'It should be. They reckon there are nearly 300,000 Germans in the pocket and the Luftwaffe can't fly in enough supplies, not in the Russian winter.'

'So Paulus will surrender?'

'I'm sure he wants to. The trouble is Hitler doesn't want

him to. Just as Stalin didn't want Chuikov to.'

'But Stalin was right, wasn't he.'

'Oh yes,' Razin said. 'He was right. No doubt about that. Ask the corpses lying in the ruins.'

Antonov said to the nurse: 'I think it's time for me to take my pills.'

She glanced at her watch.

'Oh yes, so it is.' She handed him two tablets, one white and one yellow, gave him a glass of water and took his temperature and pulse.

Then she said to Razin: 'Come on, let's celebrate,' and led the way through the screens.

***

By day Antonov listened to the radio. Patriotic music, concerts, readings from Ehrenburg, Simonov's poetry, news bulletins – belated in the case of Stalingrad – exhortations to work and fight and, a couple of times, repeats of *The Oath of the Defenders of Stalingrad* sent to Stalin and published on the eve of the 25th anniversary of the Revolution.

In sending you this letter from the trenches, we swear to you, dear Iossif Vissarionvich, that to the last drop of blood, to the last breath, to the last heart-beat, we shall defend Stalingrad . . . We swear that we shall not disgrace the glory of Russian arms and shall fight to the end. Under your leadership our fathers won the battle of Tsaritsyn. Under your leadership we shall win the great Battle of Stalingrad.

Once Antonov would have been stirred by the message. Or believed he was stirred. No longer. The words had marched from a parade-ground, disciplined and uniformed. Now he had seen sacrifice: it was necessary not glorious.

But Stalin's own words on the following day, November 7, had quickened the pulse. *There will be a holiday in our street, too.* How it had intrigued everyone. Was there at last to be a victory? Not merely a successful rearguard action?

Stalingrad had been the *holiday in our street*.

At night, between jagged dreams, Antonov listened to the

125

cold crackling outside the hospital. Cold, that was, by local definition.

When he was a boy the Antonov household had once been visited by an exuberant uncle who lived in Yakutia in Siberia, the coldest inhabited part of the world where temperatures of minus fifty degrees centigrade were not uncommon.

When he talked about the cold it became a rogue. It snapped steel bars, froze the earth hundreds of metres deep all the year round and exploded trees – 'Just like that, crash,' clapping his hands together with a report that Yury had never been able to emulate.

To thwart the rogue he had drunk spirit, pure grain spirit also known as White Dynamite, and escaped from its breath, called People's Mist because it was frozen vapour from humans, into the Red Star Dance Hall. He didn't seem to be hostile to the cold for these diversions.

'Give in to it,' he would say, 'and it kills your flesh in seconds.' The idea of murdered flesh had fascinated Yury.

Cold? In Stalingrad, currently sheathed in twenty degrees of frost, they had never been personally acquainted with the rogue. But what if you were a German without winter clothing? What if you were Meister? Antonov stared through the window at the darkness beyond the fingers of snow in the corners of the frames. He shivered and turned into his pillows.

***

The footsteps on the flagstones of the field hospital, a converted collective farm two kilometres from the Volga, rang with authority, tapping small chords of pain in Antonov's skull.

The screens parted and Razin's nurse said: 'You've got visitors,' resolutely unimpressed by their identity.

General Vasili Chuikov and a captain, bringing with them a whiff of battle, sat on chairs beside Antonov's bed and regarded him critically. Finally, Chuikov, pugilist's face drained, sores on his hands bandaged, said: 'Are they treating

126

you well?'

Antonov said they were.

Chuikov stretched his hand across the bed to the captain, a young man with grey hair. 'Give me the report.'

He scanned the hand-written document, then said: 'You've had a hard time, comrade. How do you feel now?'

'Much better, Comrade General.'

'Good. It would be a terrible thing if your talents had been destroyed by one of our own rockets.' Chuikov, running one hand through his soft bush of black hair, returned to the report. 'You nearly drowned. You owe your life to your protector.'

'Razin?' Antonov frowned.

'Of course.' Chuikov looked puzzled. 'He gave you artificial respiration. He was barely conscious when he was brought here. Didn't you know about that?'

'He didn't tell me.'

'There are men like that. Enigmas. They become soldiers out of perversity.' Chuikov picked at one of the bandages and stared at Antonov. 'You're a strange couple. You became a soldier because you had good reflexes. Without those you'd still be working in the fields.'

Chuikov's attitude towards Antonov had softened since he had been wounded: a wound was a medal.

The captain spoke at last. 'You've heard about our victories, of course?'

'I'm not up to date.' It was three days since Razin had visited him and when he asked the nurse about him she merely smiled secretively and punched his pillows into shape.

'Paulus is trapped inside the Stalingrad pocket. He has two options: he can try and break out or he can wait to be relieved.'

'Three options,' Chuikov said. 'He can surrender.'

'He won't do that, not yet anyway.' The captain didn't smile. 'Hitler has ordered him to stay put. Stupid because he might just have spoken out. Therefore we have to consider option two. Hitler has appointed Field Marshal Eric von Manstein to organise the relief of Stalingrad.'

127

'A very good general,' Chuikov said. 'As generals go.' He smiled at Antonov.

'We think,' said the captain who was uncomplicated by humour, 'that the Germans will bring up Panzer units from occupied Russia and other parts of Europe and attempt to break through to Stalingrad from the south. We shall be ready for them.'

'I don't underestimate Manstein,' Chuikov said. 'His speciality is armoured breakthroughs. It was Manstein who broke through in the Ardennes and sealed the fate of the French. It was Manstein who broke through the French lines along the Somme.'

Antonov realised that Chuikov had the same respect for Manstein that he had for Meister. But why was he sharing strategy with a soldier?

Chuikov said: 'This means that, despite what Moscow may think, Soviet troops will have to be deployed to meet the threat. And that means that we, the defenders of Stalingrad, will continue to be holed up in the city with the German Sixth Army.' Chuikov paused, listening to the sound of suffering on the other side of the screens. 'Before the Soviet counter-offensive we received a message from Moscow.' Chuikov handed Antonov a teletype. TRUST ANTONOV WILL BE FIT AGAIN TO RESUME DUTIES AT THE EARLIEST OPPORTUNITY STOP STALIN.

Antonov handed it back to Chuikov; he couldn't think of an adequate reply.

Chuikov said: 'To tell you the truth I wasn't very interested in your duel with Meister. It was an indulgence for which I had no time. But now things are different. The focus of attention has shifted from inside the city and my men, still fighting, still starving, still dying, may think they've been forgotten. So you see, Comrade Antonov, they need a fillip – something more heady than the destruction of a cellar, the capture of a pile of rubble.' Chuikov leaned towards the bed. 'Now *I* want you to kill Meister.' He held up the teletype. 'At the earliest opportunity.'

The captain took a black fountain pen from the pocket of

his brown jacket and held it up. 'How many pens?'

Antonov stared at the pen. His concentration broke it in two. 'It is a little indistinct.'

Reading from the medical report, Chuikov said: 'We were wondering if your double-vision was any better.'

'It's better,' Antonov told him.

'How many generals do you see?'

'One.'

'Thank God for that.'

Antonov, turning on his pillows, saw two captains. They said: 'Of course it is very difficult for a specialist to know whether a patient is suffering from double vision. To an extent he has to rely on the patient's word.'

That angered Antonov as nothing had angered him before. 'Are you trying to suggest . . .'

'. . . that you're malingering?' Chuikov shook his pugilist's head. 'Captain Ostrov's strong suite isn't diplomacy. Rest assured I think no such thing. All that worries me is your appetite.'

'Appetite, Comrade General?'

'For the duel. Have you lost it?'

Antonov said he hadn't and, hearing the lie in his voice, wondered if Chuikov had heard it too.

Chuikov stood up abruptly. 'We must get back to Stalingrad. At least it isn't so dangerous crossing the Volga these days: the Luftwaffe and the German gunners have other matters on their minds.' He placed a bandaged hand on Antonov's shoulder. 'Get well soon, comrade. And when you re-cross the river bring your appetite with you.'

The captain parted the screens and Chuikov, footsteps crisp on the flagstones, led the way back to battle.

That night Antonov dreamt that he and Meister, cowboy and bandit, or it might have been the other way round, were facing each other, hands on their gun holsters, in the dusty main street of an American prairie town. But when he went for his pistol he found that he could barely lift it and when he did manage to level it there were two Meisters in his sights and when he pulled the trigger he shot between the two heads of

Meister and his brother Alexander reared up with a neat hole between his eyes.

CHAPTER FIFTEEN

'Sunday was the best time in Berlin,' Lanz said one day in the middle of December. 'Crowds window-shopping in the Unter den Linden, bands playing, skating in the Tiergarten, würst in the street booths, a glass of *Berliner Weisse* in a bar . . .'

Lanz swallowed noisily. The menu that day in Stalingrad, known now as The Cauldron, was: Midday, rice and horse-meat; evening, eight ounces of bread, two meat balls (horse) à la Stalingrad, half an ounce of butter and *real* coffee. Extras: four ounces of bread, one ounce of boiled sweets and four ounces of chocolates; tobacco, one cigar or two cigarettes.

An illusion. Some units hadn't eaten for three days and all you could infer with any certainty from the bill of fare was that the beleaguered troops were devouring one of their means of transport, their horses.

Many horses hadn't been lucky enough to make the abrupt transition from a bullet in the brain to the stewpot. They had frozen to death in the white, ravaged countryside outside Stalingrad. When Meister and Lanz had arrived in the south-west, transferred from the city to harry the Russians fending off Manstein's relief force, some horses had still been alive, standing on three legs, waving a broken fourth limb in greeting and farewell.

From their observation post, a small pickling plant standing on a rise outside the charred remains of a wooden village, Meister could hear the sound of battle.

Strategically, he reflected, their position was curious. Here they were in German-held territory separated from another advancing German force by units of the Red Army who were retreating. Put like that it sounded as though the Germans were poised for another famous victory. The possibility was as illusory as the menu.

True the German relief force, known as Gruppe Hoth because, under Manstein's overall command, they were led by General Herman Hoth, stood a faint chance of reaching Stalingrad. They were said to have advanced fifty miles in eight days, only thirty miles short of their objective, but the whole purpose of the drive was to allow Paulus to escape and there was nothing victorious about that.

What Meister wanted to know, as did every solider trapped in The Cauldron – forty-five miles from east to west, fifteen miles from north to south – was whether Paulus would try to break out and meet Gruppe Hoth. Whether Hitler would finally authorise him to do so. Whether, even if he did, the Sixth Army, reeling from typhus as well as Soviet gunfire, supplementing its rations with rats, numbed by frostbite, would have the strength to thrust its way through the encircling Russians.

A gust of wind blew an eddy of snow into the pickling plant. Meister, wearing a camouflage jacket – Ordnance didn't seem to have grasped that in the Russian winter white made you a chameleon – shivered. The snow made a tiny drift in one corner of the store room under a row of glass jars containing cucumbers in frozen brine. They had broken a few jars and hammered the cucumbers from the ice but they had tasted of ammonia and Lanz had speculated that, before abandoning the village, the Russians had pissed in them.

Lanz had lit another of his fires. It was a poor thing, made from charred wood, but it glowed resolutely holding the frost at bay and it was a cheerful companion in adversity.

'Mind you,' Lanz said, holding mittened hands to the fire, 'there wasn't all that much to eat in Berlin even in those days. You know, we had ration cards – blue for meat, yellow for fat, white for sugar . . . But I suppose you didn't know much about ration cards.'

'I knew about them. But you're right, we had more than our fair share.'

'And a car, of course.'

Two, Meister remembered. He nodded. No need to elaborate.

'No problems with gasoline rationing?'

'I wouldn't have known about that.'

'My God, I wish I'd known about you Meisters – I would have robbed you blind.'

Lanz blinked at the fire. His face was protected by a wool face mask fashioned from a scarf and all his thoughts were in his eyes. He wore a stolen fur hat and a field-grey great-coat that was too big for him. He was comical or sinister according to his eyes.

Meister stared across the steppe. It would soon be dark. The hollows in the snow were filling with night and the sky to the west was a chilled pink. The wind, making stringed instruments of barbed wire and bent girders, played a dirge.

'Do you know when the best time to rob a house was?' Lanz asked.

'When the occupants were on holiday?'

'Wrong. That was when they removed the valuables. No, the best time was during a Party rally. Find a house owned by a Nazi big-shot and it was like picking your own pockets. While the family were listening to Hitler spouting and watching the storm troopers goose stepping, while the staff were drinking their master's booze . . . I broke into Ley's place once but I hadn't done my homework. I was disturbed by a valet who didn't drink and he chased me along a street lined with brownshirts and police. I only had a tiny car that ran on gas from a wood-burning stove and it was so slow I had to run for it. Luckily Hitler came along just then and instead of shouting, 'Stop thief,' the valet stopped and shouted '*Sieg Heil*' and I got away. So you see I've got a lot to thank the Führer for.'

'I would have caught you,' Meister said, 'and handed you over to my father.'

'Would you now?'

'Not now. My values have changed. They have to, don't they?' Meister gestured across the hibernating land that war wouldn't allow to sleep. 'I've got a lot to thank the Führer for as well.'

'Don't become a thief for God's sake.'

'There are worse occupations. It depends what you steal.'

'So when is it bad to be a thief?'

'When you're stealing young minds,' Meister said.

Distant gunfire made a summer storm on the winter horizon. Glimmers of light followed by grumbling explosions.

Lanz said: 'You're right of course. About values. About war. It legalises crime. For murder, read heroism. For theft, the fortunes of war. Makes you wonder, doesn't it, which values are the correct ones.'

'None of them, perhaps,' Antonov said.

'Come now.' Lanz threw a charred stick onto his puny fire. 'Rape, child abuse, cruelty . . . No justification for any of those.'

Meister, staring across the darkening void said: 'Those are crimes against people. Against ourselves if you like. The other crimes – murder, theft, fraud – they're offences against a code which we've compiled.'

'You should become a judge,' Lanz observed. 'Especially when I'm in the dock.'

'I couldn't be a judge. I don't even know whether we or the Russians are in the right any longer.'

'Neither,' Lanz said.

'Not even Misha knows.'

'Don't bet on it. A very demanding parent, Mother Russia. Just as demanding as a Jewish mother. If it really came to it, you versus Antonov, Germany versus Russia, he wouldn't hesitate.'

'He saved us,' Meister said.

'But where is he now?'

'With his own people,' Meister said. 'Where else?' and wished it were not so.

***

The dawn was dove-grey and pink-breasted, deceptively soft, as Lanz, riding a bicycle with a buckled front wheel, left the pickling plant to find breakfast. Before Meister returned to normal sniping duties such a foray wouldn't have been necessary because the cooks had been ordered to make sure he didn't go short of food. Now he had to make out as best he could and he was grateful that his bodyguard was a thief.

Lanz returned as the guns thirty miles away began their overture. His eyes glittered through his mask and his breath smoked and crystallised ahead of him.

Inside the pickling plant Lanz the Magician began his act. He placed his canvas bag on the table and with a flourish began to extract his 'rabbits'. A packet of salted biscuits, fragmented and speckled with mould; two shrivelled potatoes that had begun to sprout before the frost pruned them; a paper bag containing a spoonful of tea; and the finale, a can bearing the word SPAM.

'By courtesy of the Yanks,' Lanz said plunging a bayonet into the can. 'We should be grateful they're helping to feed the Ivans.'

'Where did you find it?'

'In the remains of the police-station,' Lanz said. 'Where else?'

He prised back a flap of metal skin. The flesh beneath was pink, glistening ambrosia, and its aroma made their stomachs whine.

Lanz held up one hand. 'Wait, let's be civilised. A proper meal, food *and* drink.' He filled a blackened saucepan with snow and perched it on the fire and emptied the tea into a jar. Then he eased the Spam out of the can onto a wooden plate.

'Do you think Gruppe Hoth will make it?' Meister asked. He talked to distract his attention from the tinned meat.

'If he's going to he'll have to hurry: there are only ten more shopping days till Christmas.'

The last Christmas Meister had spent in Hamburg had been in 1940. Special rations had been issued. Three eight-ounce rations per person of peas, beans and lentils; extra marmalade and sugar. It had also been announced in the Press that troops

135

at the front were to receive 100 million cigarettes, 25 million cigars and an ocean of booze.

Goering stated that a thousand Deutschmarks would be given to the child of every pilot killed in action, the money to be paid when he or she came of age, and the newspapers contained recipes for eggless and almost fatless Christmas cakes.

The Meister family, barely affected by shortages, were mightily impressed by Nazi beneficence and when, on Christmas Day, the High Command announced: 'The German air force refrained from attacks yesterday and last night and no enemy planes entered German territory,' Karl recalled reading about the Christmas Day truce in the trenches in the previous war and wondering why the soldiers who had shaken hands had returned to the business of killing each other.

But the talk among Hamburg's leading Nazis gathered around the Meister's log fire on Christmas Eve was about victory not truces. The conquest of the British, out-of-touch with reality on their offshore island, the establishment of a Thousand Year Reich.

Words shone like medals. Coloured candles spluttered on a tall tree, presents sprawled beneath it. The chiming night was a pre-victory celebration.

Hovering on the limits of the conversation, Meister heard whispers about Russia but paid little attention to them; nor, he admitted to himself waiting for the melted snow to boil, had he questioned any of the fireside boasts that evening. And he doubted whether the young German lying outside the pickling plant, feet shiny purple, face gnawed by rats, would have questioned them.

Even now bold claims were in circulation. Gruppe Hoth was storming towards Stalingrad; any day now it would link up with the Sixth Army. But the words had lost their shine. If Paulus was to meet Hoth where was his ammunition, fuel, food?

Goering who had once promised the children of dead Luftwaffe pilots a thousand Reichsmarks a day had also promised the Sixth Army 500 tons of supplies a day. But the sky had changed hands: the Stuka was no longer in command. And the Luftwaffe had been forced to deploy He-III bombers to augment Ju-52s flying supplies into Pitomnik and Gumrak airfields. Since the Russian encirclement they had to fly long distances; they were sabotaged by cold, blinded by blizzards, shot out of the skies by Soviet fighters. And when they did make it to the beleaguered airfields, they often brought useless cargoes. Rumour had it that on one occasion a Ju-52 had delivered two million French letters.

Five hundred tons a day?

Ask the troops dying of typhus or tetanus where their medicine was.

Ask the mortally wounded laid out in the cold to die outside an overcrowded hospital where the morphine was.

Ask the frost-bitten soldiers wearing wooden-soled boots stuffed with straw, blankets over their shoulders, where the winter clothes were.

Ask the cooks who had stewed the last dogs and cats, where the food was.

Ask the gunners rationed to thirty rounds a day where the bullets were.

Meister took the white cap that he had never been able to deliver from his pocket. Ask the parents of the boy and the girl on the scaffold where their children were.

***

'Is it nearly ready?' Meister stood up and stared at the Spam, juices spurting painfully in his mouth.

'Patience. You learn that waiting for the tumblers of a safe to answer you.' Carefully Lanz tipped boiling water into the jar containing the tea. 'We've got empty stomachs and if we don't wash the meat down it will bounce like hard shit on a drum.'

Meister continued to stare at the loaf of pink meat. He closed his eyes: it was a plum pudding. He smelled burning tallow from the Christmas tree candles. He smelled perfume.

He opened his eyes as Lanz hurled himself at him, knocking him through the flimsy wooden door, pulling him down onto the snow.

The explosion outraged his ears. Pushed the wooden walls of the plant into the shape of a barrel, then burst them open. Timber fell across Meister's body, the blast wrapped itself round him making him breathless, disfigured. Glass jars, still intact, still loaded with cucumbers, fell in the snow.

The quiet afterwards was intense.

Lanz, rolling clear, whispered: 'A grenade. I saw it coming through the window while your mind was in your stomach.'

Meister tried to speak but his voice had been squeezed from his throat. Lanz, pistol in hand, wriggled, belly close to the snow, to a low concrete wall around a water pump. He turned his head once, gesturing to Meister to stay where he was.

Meister watched, trying to swallow the pain in his throat. His camouflage jacket was ripped and there was blood on his hand but he didn't think he was badly hurt.

Somewhere on the other side of the shattered plant the Russians would be waiting in case there was any movement in the wreckage. A civilian storm group, probably.

A squall of snow swept across the steppe, pellets like shot. They stung Meister's face. He saw Lanz aim his pistol.

Three shots. A scream so young that Meister was prepared for what he saw. The grenadier was about fourteen. His hair had been cropped and there were traces of acne amid the fuzz on his cheeks. His eyes were open, staring sightlessly at the snow-filled sky, and on his brow there was a suggestion of puzzlement.

***

December 23. Paulus, sitting at a desk in an office below the control tower at Gumrak airfield, looked even greyer than he had at Golubinskaya; the greyness had spread from the streaks in his dark hair to the skin of his solemn face. Nevertheless he smiled at Meister who had been summoned from the south-west of The Cauldron by the officer with the bloodshot eyes.

138

'So neither you nor I has won.' The twitch beneath one eye now reached for his cheek. And he hadn't shaved; perhaps he was growing a beard.

The change in Paulus made Meister speculate how much he had altered since he had been pictured in *Signal*, dark and crisp, smiling for the photographer. The sensitivity that Elzbeth had once remarked upon must have been taken from him by Stalingrad.

'With respect, Herr General, neither of us has lost yet.'

On the tarmac outside ground-crew were unloading a tri-motored Ju-52 that had made it from a distant airfield. What had it been carrying? Dutch caps?

Paulus's smile pushed some of the greyness from his face. 'You're right, you're teaching me a lesson. The Luftwaffe *will* drop adequate supplies, Hoth *will* break through the Russian lines, I *will* break out of The Cauldron.'

Paulus stood up. He was huge. He gazed through the window at the bullet-pocked Ju-52. He was said to have idolised Hitler. Did he still?

The ground-crew worked slowly, like drunks concentrating. The aircraft and the tarmac and the shattered building beyond were sharp with cold this snowless day.

Paulus picked up a teletype from a tray and handed it to Meister who was standing at ease on the other side of the desk. 'Read that and tell me what you think.'

Meister read the signature first, GOEBBELS, then the text. UNDERSTAND SOVIET SNIPER ANTONOV HAS NOT BEEN SIGHTED FOR SEVERAL WEEKS STOP SUGGEST THAT AS HE MUST BE PRESUMED DEAD WE CLAIM MEISTER SHOT HIM STOP THIS WOULD BE JUST THE SORT OF STIMULUS THE SIXTH ARMY AND THE GERMAN PEOPLE NEED STOP LET ME HAVE YOUR COMMENTS . . .

It's words that win wars, not bullets.

'Well?'

'I don't think Antonov is dead.'

'Then why hasn't he tried to kill you?'

'Wounded, perhaps, Herr General?'

139

'Then we would look very foolish if we claimed you had shot him and the Soviet newspapers showed photographs of him very much alive.'

'Exactly, Herr General.'

'Not, of course, that the German people would ever get to hear that he was still alive'.

'But the Sixth Army would,' Meister ventured.

'I doubt very much whether the Minister for Propaganda and Public Enlightenment is particularly concerned about the Sixth Army.'

Normally cynicism no longer shocked Meister: from a general, from Paulus, it did.

Paulus lit another of his interminable cigarettes and inhaled deeply. Meister imagined smoke issuing from his mouth, nostrils and ears. His lungs were surely black by now.

Paulus said: 'What do you personally think of Herr Goebbels' suggestion?'

'I think it's immoral, Herr General.'

'So do I. I'm glad you said that: it took courage. I'm sure the Führer would have approved.'

Was Paulus bolstering his own resolve with some purpose in mind? The possibility excited Meister. He admired the big, arrogant general who was said to eat the same miserable rations as his men.

Paulus tore up the teletype and sat down on a swivel chair, occupied it, while the nerve beneath his eye performed a jig.

'Christmas in Stalingrad,' he remarked. 'Hardly a festive prospect. Do you realise that one of these days historians are going to debate why General Friedrich von Paulus decided to spend Yuletide in The Cauldron?'

Meister, flattered that Paulus was confiding in him, now more than ever suspecting an ulterior motive, said he supposed they would.

'Well first of all,' Paulus said, lighting another cigarette, 'they will have to remember that the Führer ordered me not to abandon the Stalingrad pocket. If I disobeyed Hitler then there is no reason why my officers shouldn't disobey me, no reason why the troops shouldn't disobey their officers.'

Another Ju-52 fell out of the bleak sky, found the runway, hopped along it, then leaned to one side digging a wing into the frozen mud. As it settled an ambulance and a fire tender sped across the airfield.

Paulus took little heed: a crash landing was nothing new. 'The historians,' he said, 'will also have to ask themselves whether, if I had ignored Hitler, I would have had the strength to break out. The food to sustain a long march, the amunition to feed the guns, the gasoline to fuel the mobile columns.' He lowered his head, knowing the answers.

'There is another consideration,' he said after a while, abandoning the historians. 'By holding out in Stalingrad I am tying down enemy forces which could be attacking our positions elsewhere. I am giving other German commanders breathing space, time to consolidate.'

Consolidate, Meister had learned, usually meant retreat. He said: 'May I ask a question, Herr General?'

'Of course.'

'If the Führer gave the order to break out would you do so, bearing in mind your second reason for staying put – lack of supplies.'

'We Germans are a disciplined nation which is another way of saying we are obedient.'

An orderly brought coffee. It tasted of walnuts.

'Yes,' Paulus went on, 'we would try to break out and our soldiers would fight heroically. But here in Stalingrad even greater calls are going to be made on their courage because there will be no rewards, no glory.'

'If Gruppe Hoth gets through could we escape through their bridgehead?'

'Escape? I think you mean break out.' Paulus prodded the pyramid of cigarette ends in the ash-tray with one finger. 'I thought at one stage that Hoth might make it, just as I thought that Goering would send adequate provisions. No longer. Hoth is only twenty-five miles or so away but his men are exhausted. The Russian Sixth Mechanised Corps is attacking him, Rotmistrov's Seventh Tank Corps are moving in . . .' Paulus prodded the cigarette butts once more; the pyramid

141

collapsed.

'Couldn't we go out to meet Gruppe Hoth?' *We*, the general and I, joint Sixth Army strategists!

'On foot? On horseback? Do you know the most important commodity that Junkers,' pointing at the crippled aircraft, 'has brought?' And when, although he guessed, Meister shook his head: 'The fuel in its tanks. Napoleon once said, "An army marches on its stomach." But not tanks, armoured cars, trucks . . . ' Paulus swallowed the dregs of his coffee. 'It has been hinted that I might be offered an important post in the OKW, if I break out. I'm afraid someone else is going to get that job.'

The orderly returned to remove the cups. Outside the ground crew were crawling over the stricken Junkers, ants feeding off a winged insect. One slipped on a frozen puddle and lay still for a few seconds before climbing laboriously to his feet. Meister felt suddenly cold; he swayed.

'Are you all right?'

'Yes, Herr General.' He bit the inside of his lip. Blood flowed, the cold leaked from his skull. He blamed the heat of the room after the frost. And hunger.

'You may sit down if you wish.'

'I'm all right,' Meister said.

'Then I'll stand up.' Paulus stood at the window. Staring across the steppe to Germany, Meister thought. 'You're probably wondering why a general is confiding in a private. Well, I have a very good reason: you are the only person now who can give my men – more than a quarter of a million of them – any sort of victory. So you see, I think you should know our exact position.'

Meister stared uncomprehendingly at Paulus.

'A Christmas victory,' Paulus said softly. 'That's what we need. Before I have to cut the rations again.' He picked up a typewritten sheet of paper and read from it. 'Seven ounces of horsemeat including bones; two-and-a-half ounces of bread; two-fifths of an ounce of fats; two-fifths of an ounce of sugar and one cigarette. Just one.' He stared at the cigarette smoking in his hand. 'I will eat the same as the men but I can't

142

do without my drug.'

Meister said: 'Excuse me, Herr General, but I don't under-stand.'

Paulus said: 'Antonov has re-crossed the river.'

He produced a map; an inglorious substitute for the arrow-slashed cartography that had once adorned his desk, little more than a sketch of the Russian positions huddled along the banks of the Volga inside the city and the German disposi-tions opposite them.

Paulus said: 'To think we came all that way,' removing one hand from the map and signposting Byelorussia, the Ukraine, the Kalmyk steppe, with it, 'but we couldn't take those last few metres.'

Meister waited.

Paulus said: 'The Volga froze completely on December 16 converting the Soviet positions inside the city into a front line rather than a beleaguered outpost. Supplies and reinforce-ments are reaching them by sled and lorry. Antonov crossed on December 19 and has taken up a position somewhere there.' Paulus prodded a cross on No Man's Land.

'May I ask how you know this, Herr General?'

Misha?

'That needn't concern you. But I will tell you this: there was no great secrecy involved. It was almost as if the Russians wanted us to know he had returned. Almost as if Antonov wanted you to know.'

'And you want me to go after him again?'

Paulus said: 'I want him dead by midnight on the twenty-fourth. A Christmas present for the Sixth Army.'

143

CHAPTER SIXTEEN

The Volga was peace. A broad white aisle leading to an altar of harmony. Only four days earlier it had been war. A wound running with the pus of battle. Then overnight, the ice-floes had knitted and the healing snow had fallen.

The truck taking Antonov and Razin, both in winter white, back to the west bank travelled swiftly along an ice road marked with stakes. Occasionally it skidded but the driver, a teenager with a dangerous face, laughed; it could skid all the way to Astrakhan as far as he was concerned.

Ahead lay the stumps of Stalingrad, white and gentle now. Snow fell hesitantly.

'How many Stalingrads can you see?' Razin asked massaging his arm.

The double vision had stayed with Antonov for a long time and hadn't really focussed satisfactorily when he had been discharged from the hospital but the doctors had been so sceptical that in the end he had told them what they wanted to hear.

'Only one,' he told Razin.

His eyesight was accurate most of the time; it was only when he concentrated that it multiplied.

The driver, steering with one hand, said: 'I hear you're going after the Fritz again.' The truck uprooted a stake. 'How are you going to find him?'

'He'll probably find me.'

144

The driver wound down his window and flicked a cigarette-butt through it. Cold swarmed into the cabin. Antonov pulled the hood over the thick blond stubble growing from his shaven scalp.

'Then he has the advantage?'

'Not necessarily. Not if I've got a good vantage point.'

'How do you know he'll be there?'

'I don't. But he'll be somewhere in the pocket if he hasn't been killed.'

If Meister found him he hoped it wouldn't be Misha's doing.

'Make sure you get him,' the driver said. 'Before Christmas. We need a shot in the arm now that all the death and glory boys are outside Stalingrad. What did we do? Just hung on while the vermin threw everything they'd got at us, that's all. We retreated, they're advancing. We were gallant defenders, they're fucking heroes. Yes,' the driver said, swinging the truck into a ponderous skid to avoid an on-coming sledge, 'you get him, I'll be the first to shake your hand.'

'Christmas?' Razin said. 'What's this talk about Christmas? It's a heathen festival. Be patient, wait until the New Year. Celebrate his victory,' clumping Antonov on the shoulder, 'with Grandfather Frost and the Snow Maiden.'

'Christmas is Christmas,' the driver said. 'You know that. By God the *zakuski* we used to have at home at Christmas. Caviar, black and red, smoked salmon, *pirozhki* . . . and firewater, vats of it.' He pursed his lips and blew as though he were exhaling flames.

'And the food in Stalingrad now?' Razin asked.

'Not bad compared with the shit we were eating. Meat, fish, potatoes. The cooks position their stews so that the wind takes the smell into the Fritz lines. You can hear their stomachs rumbling a kilometre away. And yet they still fight as if their bellies were full of bullets.'

'You haven't eaten,' Razin announced, 'until you've tasted *manti*. Dumplings filled with spiced meat and onions. Now that's food. A Kirghiz dish,' he informed them.

145

Antonov said: 'So the little nurse from Frunze is a good cook as well?'

'As well as what? As a matter of fact, when all this is over we're going to get married.'

'Congratulations. Will she mind being married to a soldier?'

'My time's almost up. When we've chased the vermin back to Berlin I'm going to become a civilian again. And study law again,' he said almost shyly. Antonov noticed that the ragged ends of his moustache had been trimmed.

'Where do you come from?' Antonov asked the driver. But he never found out because snow distorts distance and here they were on the west bank, beside a red flag as bright as a poppy. Back in the battlefield.

***

Chuikov's headquarters had been transformed. It was surrounded by a barbed-wire fence, the corrugated iron roof of each dug-out was numbered in black paint and paths had been cut through the trampled snow.

Antonov was escorted to dugout No. 14 where the captain with the young face and old hair and Gordov, the storm group leader, were waiting for him. Gordov looked plumper, as though the hunting had been good, and his pet beard was glossy. He even seemed pleased to see Antonov.

'Welcome back to active service,' he said.

The dugout was heated by a one bar electric fire that had made a collection of toasted bread-crumbs; grey blankets, German by the look of them, covered the walls. In Stalingrad this was luxury and the occupants, drinking tea served from a battered samovar, glowed with it and it was difficult to believe that the Germans were only a few hundred metres away.

The captain handed Antonov a glass of tea. It was sharp with lemon. How had they managed to get hold of a lemon? The captain held up a small bottle labelled LEMON CONCENTRATE.

146

He said: 'Are you glad to be back?' tone suggesting that he was a hard man to convince and, when Antonov said, truthfully, that he was: 'The odds will be against Meister this time: you're refreshed, he will be exhausted.'

Antonov said: 'With respect, Comrade Captain, I didn't know the odds had previously been in Meister's favour.'

'I didn't say they were. But he's a trained marksman not a hunter from the taiga.'

Antonov knowing that he was invaluable and experiencing an unaccustomed surge of power, said: 'May I ask, Comrade Captain, where you were born?'

The captain said: 'Minsk,' scarcely the Paris of the Soviet Union. And hurriedly: 'You've brought your appetite for the duel back with you?' Chuikov's turn of phrase, Antonov recalled.

'I don't want to kill Meister if that's what you mean.'

The silence was a fog. Antonov heard the scrape of shovel on concrete outside it. It thickened, then evaporated.

Gordov found direction first. 'Then why are you here? Why did my men sacrifice their lives to rescue you, take you across the river?' Astonishment being forged into anger.

'I didn't say I wouldn't kill Meister; I said I didn't want to.'

The captain said: 'Do you want me to tell General Chuikov that?'

'If you wish, Comrade Captain,' Antonov replied. 'But please convey my message accurately – didn't want to, not wouldn't.'

The captain drank some tea, small precise sips. He was a precise man, Antonov decided, confused by non-conformity. When his glass was empty he said: 'Tell us why you don't want to kill Meister.'

'Why should I want to kill him?'

'Because he's a German,' Gordov said. 'Vermin.'

'I've got nothing against him personally.'

'What would happen if we all thought that way?'

'We wouldn't have wars,' Antonov said.

'We didn't start this one,' Gordov said. 'Do you want the Germans to march right through Russia to the Sea of Japan?'

'The war,' Antonov said, astonishing himself, 'was started by old men. Meister and I are young. Maybe if we were all taught when we were young that there is no need to fight each other then we'd live in peace.'

'Take a look at any playground,' Gordov said. 'Boys fight.'

'Because they copy their fathers.'

The captain said: 'I'm sure General Chuikov will be interested in your views.'

But Antonov, battle-wise, knew he wouldn't tell him: it was the captain's job to pit him against Meister and Chuikov wouldn't want complications.

Gordov said: 'My sister was killed by the vermin.'

'I'm sorry,' Antonov said. 'Truly sorry. But a lot of German girls will die before the war is over.'

'Have you seen what the Germans did in the countryside? Have you seen the bodies of innocent peasants massacred in the villages?'

Antonov said: 'I just don't want it to ever happen again. Is that so wrong?'

Gordov made a grab for Antonov's rifle. 'Here, give me that. I don't trust you.'

But the captain reached it first. 'Don't be stupid, you haven't got his eyes.' And to Antonov: 'Dangerous talk, comrade. I would curb that tongue of yours if I were you.'

'I don't pull the trigger with my tongue, Comrade Captain.'

'Are you sure you're going to pull it?'

'If I don't Meister will pull his.'

This seemed to satisfy the captain because when Gordov, furiously combing his beard with his fingers, tried to speak he held up his hand. 'Let's get down to business,' he said.

He spoke in numbers. The ruins of a wooden church 300 metres from the dugout. A reconnaissance party leaving at 1400 hours. Antonov to follow accompanied by Razin and two others. The captain treasured numbers.

'It will still be light at 1400 hours,' Antonov said.

'So?'

Gordov said: 'There's a culvert leading from here to the edge of the graveyard beside the church. I know, I helped to

148

build it.' He frowned, displeased at the intrusion of the period before he became a warrior.

'We want to make sure that Meister knows where you are,' the captain said. 'Then, when he comes for you, it will be easy for you, in a vantage point, wearing winter-white, to put a bullet between his eyes.'

Antonov said: 'Can you tell me, Comrade Captain, how you're going to make sure Meister knows where I am?'

'Because we have a courier,' the captain said, opening the door and calling Misha's name.

***

Snipers, like hunters, anticipate deceit and, defensively, call it strategy. Antonov anticipated the captain. And deceived him.

Claiming that he had been told to report to the medical officer for a last check-up, he went looking for Misha and found him in a corner of the improvised canteen drinking a glass of hot milk.

Since the Russian victories some of his lost boyhood had returned to his face, blunting the sharp angles, but he was still bird-bright and wary.

Sitting in front of him at a trestle table, Antonov said: 'Why, Misha? You don't want me to kill Meister.'

'Our soldiers need a victory. General Chuikov said so. He told the captain to tell me that. It's Christmas . . . '

'And Christmas for the German soldiers.'

'I'm Russian.' Misha made a hole in the skin of the milk with a teaspoon. 'So are you.'

'But you like Meister.'

Misha stared intently into the hole in the skin. 'One of you has got to die,' he said, eventually. 'I had hoped – ' He drank the milk, leaving the skin on the inside of the glass.

'That it was all over?' Antonov felt very old. 'Life isn't as convenient as that. Perhaps you and I, our generation, no your generation . . . ' The words were trapped butterflies. He asked gently: 'Where have you got to tell Meister I will be?'

149

'In a house, No. 23, at the edge of a graveyard beside a church.'

'Ah.' Antonov digested the captain's lie. 'And from the church a sniper would have a good view of that house?'

Misha nodded.

'And a good view of another sniper creeping up to the house?'

'I suppose so, yes.'

'I won't be in that house,' Antonov said. 'They want to make it easy for me, Misha.'

'They could have told me.' Misha made a railway line with a fork on the soft-wood surface of the table. 'My parents used to say things that weren't quite true.'

'But I don't expect they were lies, not real ones.'

'People used to come into the bakery and they would be nice to them. Make jokes with them. Then, when they'd gone they would say bad things about them.'

'But they were being kind to them,' Antonov said as echoes of his own childhood reached him. 'If you think about it they were being kind.'

'I suppose so,' Misha said.

'You know you've got to tell Meister where I really am?'

'Then he might kill you.'

'One of us has to die. You said that. And it has to be fair.'

'I don't think my parents meant to say bad things about them,' Misha said. 'They liked them really.'

'You'll tell him where I really am?'

'I'll speak to him,' Misha said but Antonov wasn't sure what he wanted him to say.

CHAPTER SEVENTEEN

Inside the grand scheme of things, inside Stalingrad where they had defied the Germans since the long-ago summer, what was left of the Russian 62nd Army took small bites out of the enemy. A shattered workshop, a ravaged recreation ground, the shell of a restaurant, the stump of a pump-house . . . But the Germans clutched their captured rubble tightly; within the encircling Russians they still held most of the city, still bitterly contested a work-bench or an inspection pit in a demolished factory to the north.

Near Tsaritsa Gorge, in the school playground where they had been holed up before the Russian offensive, Meister and Lanz, standing beneath a numbed sky, peered over the wall and surveyed the debris where half a million souls had once lived.

Lanz said: 'We hang on like ticks on a dog.'

'Like those,' said Meister, pointing at the two shrivelled pears still hanging on the bare limbs of the tree. 'Our Christmas decorations,' he added.

It was nine o'clock on the morning of Christmas Eve, a Thursday, and hostilities were sporadic. Mortar shells exploded and machine-guns coughed but the noise was bandaged with cold. In Hamburg, Meister's mother would be fretting about festive meals and his father would be worrying about how many high-ranking Nazis would materialise that evening, and in her small apartment Elzbeth would be burrowing into sleep after a night-shift in the factory where, against her parents' wishes, she now worked.

Meister felt her warmth, her back pressed into his chest. He slid his arms around her and cupped her breasts and kissed her open lips as she turned to him. He thought it would be tragic if he died before he had made love to her.

Lanz fished the two model soldiers he had taken from the toy factory from his pocket. 'Perhaps I'll give them to him for his birthday,' he said. 'It's tomorrow really but we celebrate it on June the twenty-fourth, Midsummer's Day, so he can have two lots of presents.'

'How old is he?' Meister asked. 'You never told me about him.'

'Eight tomorrow.'

'Does he live in Berlin?' Lanz's private life had always been under lock and key.

'On the banks of the Spree.' Lanz hesitated. 'He lives with his mother. She's a school teacher.' For Lanz this was expansive; Christmas had turned the key. 'I wanted to marry her but she said she wouldn't marry a thief and I said it was the only job I knew and we had lots of rows about it and I thought, "Shit, if we're fighting already maybe it's better that we don't get married," and we never did. But she writes to me; at least I used to get letters until I came to this *arshloch* of a place. I've got them here.' He slid one hand inside his greatcoat.

'Maybe she would marry a soldier, a corporal.'

'So who's going to stay in the Army?' Cautiously, Lanz entered a minefield of words. 'Since I came to Stalingrad I've been thinking about settling down. You know, you start to think how short and sweet life is and if I'm lucky enough to get out of here alive why should I risk going to prison?' Lanz now spoke with extreme caution. 'As a matter of fact I've written to her along those lines.'

'What would you do?' Meister asked.

'Security,' Lanz told him. 'Set a thief to catch a thief.' He examined the toy soldiers; each was standing to attention holding his rifle. 'Midsummer's Day. We'll be split up by then, you and I, because you won't need a nursemaid

152

anymore but you might like to think about the boy with his soldiers.'

'What's his name?' Meister asked.

'Karl,' Lanz said. 'Maybe that's why I've looked after you so well.'

A voice from the classroom called out for water. There were two soldiers there, lying beside the fire. One was suffering from typhus, the other from tetanus. They had been left there to die.

It was the soldier suffering from typhus, spread by lice and rampaging through the Sixth Army, who wanted water. His temperature was soaring, there were red blotches on his wrists and his eyes deep in his face were staring at death.

Lanz gave him water in a tin mug. The other soldier watched. He hadn't yet glimpsed death but the tetanus spasms were under way and he had difficulty in opening his jaws.

Misha came into the playground as three Ilyushin dive-bombers swept across the sky. He brought with him a tin of condensed milk, black bread and smoked fish.

Meister welcomed him joyously: even Lanz was pleased to see him, but, through Meister, he still asked penetrating questions. 'Ask him why he's still allowed to wander inside the German lines?'

'Because I bring food,' Misha said. 'Don't you want any?'

'Ask him if he wants a cuff round the ears for being cheeky.' Lanz raised his arm; he hadn't tied the ear-flaps of his fur hat and when he moved they trembled.

Misha wore a black, peaked cap, a blue reefer that stretched to his knees and grey trousers rolled around his ankles. Meister had at last agreed to wear a fur hat acquired by Lanz but he refused to lower the ear-flaps: if his hearing was impaired his other senses would suffer too.

Lanz said: 'What happens when he returns to the Russian lines? Don't they ask what he's been doing over here?'

'I go straight to headquarters,' Misha told Meister. 'I bring them information instead of food. Like other boys.'

'And the information. Is it true or false?' Meister asked.

'It's true. But what does it matter?'

And that was true, too. What did it matter anymore? Gruppe Hoth was retreating and the Sixth Army was trapped and that was all there was to it; nothing Misha could tell the Russians would make any difference.

They opened the can of condensed milk and broke the bread and leathery fish into pieces. Meister tried to feed the sick men but they had no appetite.

Meister chewed some fish, then asked the question he had been nursing. 'Do you know where Antonov is?'

He and Lanz had come to the playground calculating that, if, as Paulus had suggested, the Russians wanted them to find Antonov they would send Misha there.

Misha sucked the thick, sweet milk from his finger. Then hesitantly, he delivered what sounded like a rehearsed answer: 'I can take you to him,' in the same tone that he must have used in reply to a question in the classroom.

Lanz's words of counsel earlier that morning came back to Meister. 'I know he saved our lives once but that doesn't mean you can trust him. If this thing with you and Antonov is heading for a showdown one of you is going to get killed and, although Misha has taken a shine to you, he's got to choose one way or the other and he is Russian. So make sure he doesn't lead you into a trap.'

Meister said: 'I asked you where Antonov is?'

'Between the German and Russian lines. One of those positions that's Russian one minute, German the next.'

'What is it now?' Meister asked.

'Nobody's.'

Lanz asked: 'What's he saying?' and when Meister told him: 'Ask him where the cover is. Factory, store, warehouse, a pile of bricks . . . ' but when Meister asked Misha all he said was: 'I can take you there.'

'Then it's a trap,' Lanz said, rolling a piece of black bread into a pellet and popping it into his mouth.

'I don't think so.'

'You mean you don't want to think so.'

Meister addressed Misha, moulding his words with great

154

care. 'All right, lead us there. But don't forget that neither of us wants to kill each other. But, as we have to, everything must be equal. Do you understand that?'

The gold watch chimed deep inside Misha's clothing. 'I understand,' he said.

'I must know the real place where Antonov is waiting and he must know that I know.'

Misha said: 'I can take you there.' He turned, hands thrust in his pockets, shoulders slightly hunched, and walked through the classroom and out of the door beyond the fire, and for a moment he was a nine-year-old schoolboy on his way home on a cold winter's day.

As he stood waiting outside a wind loaded with snow bowled through the ruins, found the school and shook the pear tree divesting it of one of its decorations. The shrivelled pear bounced once, then lay still.

Picking up his rifle, Meister, accompanied by Lanz, followed Misha, leaving the two soldiers to die.

***

Often white-clad Russians inside The Cauldron attacked during a snowstorm; they did so as Meister, Lanz and Misha reached a German command post, a cellar protected by a cluster of foxholes and a crippled tramcar.

As grenades tumbled out of the snow, as ghosts uttered jackal war cries, Meister and Lanz dived behind the tramcar pulling Misha with them. A German machine-gun chattered. A white figure reared up, one hand clawing the red patch on his chest. Fragmentation grenades exploded. One rolled towards Meister; he stared at it fascinated. Swearing, Lanz grabbed it and hurled it away; it exploded above them, cubes of cast-iron thudding into the ground and striking the snow-pasted sides of the tramcar.

Meister told Misha not to move; then he climbed inside the tram, levelled his rifle through a broken window beside the driver's controls, and shot a Russian through the head. He fired again, twice, on target both times.

155

How many more of them? The white-clad soldiers, bayonets drawn, had already taken two foxholes; behind them came the mainstay of the attack, troops wearing fur hats and brown padded jackets. Meister shot two of them.

In the next foxhole bayonets flashed. In, out. He didn't know whether he would have the courage to face a thrusting blade. Or to wield one. Stalemate. Until *he* killed you.

A Russian knelt, aiming his rifle at the tramcar and Meister shot him seeing, as he squeezed the trigger, a target with black circles round a bullseye. Beside the tram, Lanz was firing his pistol.

As always the Russians attacked with little regard for their own lives – Meister didn't believe there was anything to choose between the courage of Russians and Germans – but they had to minimise losses and suddenly Meister realised they were concentrating on the firepower from the tramcar.

Snow fell softly in Christmas flakes.

Meister, re-loading his rifle, turned and found he was sharing the tramcar with a Russian soldier.

They stared at each other. The Russian was young, about his own age. The ear-flaps of his fur hat were tied above his head. His face was lean and wild. Meister could smell him. Vodka and tobacco and, despite the cold, sweat. Meister was terrified of the bayonet, its nakedness. But the terror was guiding him; avoid the thrusting blade, hit back somehow. So there wasn't much difference between fear and courage, he thought, as he prepared to pull back the rifle from the window, swing it round and shoot.

If one of them spoke maybe the need to kill would disappear. He opened his mouth but no words emerged. The Russian moved towards him. He looked like a student Meister had known in Hamburg.

As Meister flung himself to one side, swivelling his rifle, the Russian lunged with his bayonet. The blade buried itself in the varnished wood beside the driver's seat.

The Russian pulled the rifle. The bayonet began to come loose.

Meister levelled his rifle at the Russian. They looked at

each other. The Russian had thick eyebrows that almost joined each other.

Meister wished they could talk.

He took first pressure on the trigger.

The Russian spat.

Turning, Meister clubbed him on the head with the butt of the rifle. As he climbed from the tramcar he felt as though he were alighting outside Hamburg's rathaus.

By which time German re-inforcements had arrived and the Russians were retreating into the falling snow.

***

What was left of the bathhouse, the meeting place of the Soviet male, lay between Mamaev Hill and the chemical factory amid a confusion of twisted railway lines leading nowhere.

Although devastated, it still retained traces of nobility and hints of decadence. Like a Roman ruin, Meister thought. Marble benches climbed from either side of a miniature amphitheatre; a brass rail, fragile with wear, swung in the breeze; steps led down into darkness that was surely scented.

Here, on the benches, while steam issued from pipes attached to the walls, convivial men had met to talk and share and boast and argue and beat each other as pink as prawns with birch twigs before retiring to the rest-room to drink beer, eat salted fish, play chess and continue the debate.

Situated on a rise, it was a perfect look out post. What's more it was only 800 metres from the vantage point where, according to Misha, Antonov was waiting.

Meister, standing in the small arena of the steam-room, called out to Misha but there was no reply.

***

While Meister explored sniping possibilities, Lanz disappeared into the darkness below the stairs. A scrape of a match followed by a spurt of light and the glow of candle-light.

Another matchscrape and Meister smelled wood-smoke ascending the stairs.

He sat on a slab of masonry and peered through a crack in the wall. Snow fell lightly on him through the space where the roof had been. He could just see the ruins of a church, a cemetery containing graves demarcated by what looked like brass bedsteads, beyond it the remains of a house.

After a while he heard a bird singing. For a moment he thought the song must be in his head. He called to Lanz: 'Can you hear anything?' and when Lanz said yes, a bird singing, he went to look for it.

In the rest-room where, mugs of beer in their hands, Russians had once recovered from the masochism of the steam-room, he had to light a match because here the roof was intact. Wooden chess pieces were scattered over the floor. Among them lay the body of a Russian soldier, his body preserved by the cold, a pool of frozen blood beside him.

Above him, in a cage suspended from the ceiling, a canary was singing to itself. Who had owned the canary and what was it doing in the bathhouse? Perhaps the soldier who had been shot in the chest had found it in an abandoned house and brought it with him.

A packet of birdseed stood on a stone-topped bar where beer had once been dispensed. Meister poured a handful of seed into the cage: Antonov would have done the same.

Then he returned to the steam-room and, through the sights of the Karabiner, gazed steadily at the shell of the wooden church.

CHAPTER EIGHTEEN

From the church Antonov saw grey smoke rising from the broken chimney of the bathhouse. He saw it as a smoke signal I AM HERE.

The wind had dropped and the smoke was a stem in the sky and the unpredictable day was blue and gold and white, a traitress diverting attention from the truth, the cold. Not cold, according to Antonov – about minus twenty-five degrees he guessed; cold enough to freeze your soul according to Razin, delicate city dweller.

And such was the prevalent splendour of this day, that it found beauty, bare and lonely, in the devastated landscape. A leafless tree bowed eloquently by an explosion, a wall sculptured by shell-bursts; even corpses wearing shrouds of snow were invested with dignity.

Antonov, white hood over his corn-stubble hair, walked round the nave of the church. It was open to the sky and it smelled of charred wood. He had glanced into a church once in Novosibirsk and had been surprised to see so many old women praying; he had been impressed, for he was very young at the time, by the priest's beard because it looked as though it had been knitted.

On the blackened wall he noticed an icon. Heat had partially melted the face of Christ on the cross but the eyes were still questing. He felt a great temptation to pray but, because religion had been outside the curriculum of his

159

school, he didn't quite know how. Or to whom.

Then suddenly as the sun gilded the remains of the altar, sacrificed to war, he understood. Communism, Christianity, Mohammedism . . . it didn't matter to whom you prayed, only that you prayed. And he prayed. For Meister and himself.

***

In the vestry, a stone extension of the church and still intact, Razin was sitting on a pile of dusty vestments writing a letter to the nurse.

'She says she's quite happy to live in Kiev,' he said as Antonov walked in. 'I thought you were supposed to be keeping watch?'

'No point. Neither of us will show ourselves and neither will make a move outside until it starts to snow.'

'And then?'

'There's a wrecked tank out here, a KV. I want you to draw his fire while I make a run for it. With luck I should be able to pick him off from behind it.'

'Maybe he thinks you're in the house. If he does he'll be looking the wrong way and you might get a sighting from here.'

'He knows we're here.'

'You're very sure of the boy,' Razin said, signing his letter with a flourish.

'You have to trust someone.'

Antonov looked through a small, barred window framed with shards of glass. The sky was still blue and there was the Russian tank, an impotent prehistoric animal, abandoned among the mangled rail tracks.

A hundred metres past it stood a heavy German anti-tank gun. It had been punched on its side and its blunt muzzle was burried in the snow.

Razin said: 'When you go watch out for anti-personnel mines. They've got three copper whiskers. Tread on those and Meister won't have a target any more and he wouldn't

160

want that, would he?' He looked at Antonov curiously. 'Now that it's inevitable, what do you feel?'

'The same as I always did: I don't want to kill him.'

'And he feels the same way?'

'I don't know how he feels.'

'But you think you know.'

'I should like to have met him in Hamburg,' Antonov said. 'In an inn maybe with his friends. His girl-friend perhaps.'

'How do you know he's got one?'

'That girl in the photograph in the German magazine. But as he's rich and smart and clever he's probably got lots of girls.'

'Will you marry Tasya?'

'Not now, Stalingrad has re-arranged our lives.'

'It brought you close together on the east bank. You can't get much closer than that.'

'You don't know what happened over there.'

'You didn't spent the time discussing Marxism,' Razin said.

'In any case, what's the point of discussing the future? There is no future for one of us, Meister or me. One of us will never even know the outcome of the war.'

'We'll win,' Razin said. 'Russia and her enemies will win.'

'Enemies?'

'Have you forgotten? Before Germany attacked us Britain and America were our enemies. Imperialists, capitalists. It's only the Germans who have made them our allies.'

'Do you think they will become enemies again when all this is over?'

'It's a possibility,' Razin said. He picked up the rifle he had brought with him from the east bank and began to clean it. 'A distinct possibility.'

'You make it sound as if we're fighting for nothing.'

'We fought,' Razin said, 'because we had to.'

'I would like to think there was some glory in it somewhere.'

Razin said: 'Glory is for gravestones.'

'Maybe we're fighting to end all wars. Maybe people will look back upon Stalingrad and think, "Nothing was worth

161

that. Nothing like that must ever happen again."'

'Or maybe they'll say, "Stalingrad? Where was that? What happened there?"'

'I want to believe that I've got to kill Meister for a reason.'

Razin leaned his rifle against the wall. 'You're forcing my hand,' he said. 'The important thing is that there isn't any reason: you don't want to kill each other.'

Antonov gazed into a time when there was no war and saw Meister sitting in an inn covered with an envelope of snow. He was drinking beer from a tankard and smiling at the girl in the photograph. He looked closer and the young man wasn't Meister, it was himself.

***

Lanz emerged from the rest-room of the bathhouse carrying the dead soldier's rifle. It was an SVT1938 fitted with a telescopic sight; the soldier had been a sniper too.

He sat close to the pipes on the wall, hissing with steam since he had lit the boiler downstairs, and examined it.

Meister, sitting half way down the tier of marble benches, said: 'They did away with those last year. They were too light, too fragile.'

'But pretty,' Lanz said, running his finger along the cleaning rod fitted to the side of the stock instead of underneath it. He lit a Russian cigarette, a Kazbeck, and inhaled, grimacing. 'So which of you is going hunting?'

'Whoever makes a move becomes a target. Even if it's snowing.'

'You or him?'

'Both of us?'

'Well for God's sake get it over with,' Lanz said. 'This is no way to spend Christmas Eve.'

'You wanted to stretch it out not so long ago.'

'And now I want an end to it. An end to the siege. An end to the war. Goodbye Russia. Hallo Berlin.'

Meister said: 'It's funny, you know. I keep thinking, "One of us has got to die." But that isn't true, is it? Both of us could die.'

He moved closer to the steam, feeling it warm and wet on his cheeks. If I get back to Germany, he thought, I will go hunting like Antonov. Stalk game beneath a vault of pine trees. Take with me bread and cheese and fruit. And he thought how fine it would be if they could go hunting together, he and Antonov; how fine it would be to adjourn afterwards to an inn and drink beer together and discuss what they had or hadn't shot.

The bird sang daintily.

The steam, thicker now, formed sparkling clouds above the bathhouse.

The sky began to grow heavy with snow.

***

Observing the heaviness, Antonov said: 'It will snow again soon.'

'The sooner the better,' Razin said.

'Then I will make my move.'

Antonov stared through the barred window. The tank, even though it was tipped forward on its tracks, had assumed an air of menace.

As he stared the outline of the tank began to lose its definition; then there were two tanks.

***

Meister crawled to the top bench and peered through a gap in the jagged rim of the retaining wall. He saw a knocked-out Russian tank. Between the bathhouse and the tank stood a big German anti-tank gun. For several minutes he lay considering the gun and its formidable armour.

***

Misha arrived in the church as the first flakes of snow were falling. The peak of his cap was dusted white and his cheeks were polished.

163

He joined them in the vestry and sat on the vestments beside Razin.

He said: 'I told Meister where you are.' His breath steamed.

'The truth?' Antonov asked.

'The truth. Like you told me to. He wanted the truth too. He said everything had to be equal. I understand that. But I don't understand why you have to kill each other. I did once. Not any more.'

His voice was fluted with anxiety.

Antonov wanted to explain but there wasn't any reason. Because he's German and I'm Russian? What sort of answer was that? He told Misha that after the war such questions might have answers; that the war was being fought to settle such questions.

And he thought: Meister and I understand why we *don't* have to kill each other. But it was too late for that: it always had been.

Antonov said to Misha: 'I have to go any moment now.'

But Misha didn't reply. He just stood, shoulders slightly hunched, staring at Antonov as, rifle gripped in one hand, he prepared to make a run for the marooned tank.

***

In the bath-house Meister prepared to make a run for the anti-tank gun. It was too soon to make his move, he knew that. The snow wasn't thick enough and he would be visible, black on white, like a target propelled across the range in Hamburg; but he had to go now; had to.

He told Lanz to keep him covered with the dead Russian's rifle.

Lanz, kneeling below the top bench, said: 'Give it a couple of minutes. If Antonov's still in the church he'll put a bullet through your brains before you're half way there.' His bald patch was spreading with snow.

Meister buttoned up his camouflage jacket, picked up the Karabiner. 'I'm going now,' he said.

164

'Stupid.'

Meister smelled perfume.

'Tell him one of the toy soldiers was from me,' he said and was gone.

***

Razin said: 'If he's got any sense he'll still be in the bathhouse and he'll see you because the snow isn't thick enough yet.'

He pulled the white hood back from his head. His neat moustache was a stranger in his crumpled features.

'Sense?' Antonov came out of the vestry into the shell of the nave. 'Since when has sense entered this business?'

Razin picked up his rifle and stood behind a jigsaw stretch of wall beside the altar.

Antonov turned to say goodbye to Misha but he had gone.

He said to Razin: 'Two shots. Now.'

And ran from the church. Too soon, he thought as the sparse flakes of snow touched his face. Like an animal in the taiga that, in old age, has grown careless.

***

From his position near the altar Razin fired two shots. Lanz, sighting him from the top of the steam-room, picked him off with one bullet. Razin's dying shot, before he fell beside the altar, hit Lanz in the head, knocking him down the benches to the floor of the small amphitheatre where once men had attacked each other with nothing more lethal than birch-twigs.

***

As petals of snow began to cover their bodies Antonov came from behind the tank. Meister from behind the gun.

They stared at each other.

A canary sang.

A gold watch chimed.

165

They turned and looked at Misha standing between them.
Then they dropped their rifles.

EPILOGUE

Hitler promoted Paulus to Field Marshal at the end of January, 1943; almost immediately afterwards Paulus surrendered. All German resistance within the Stalingrad pocket ended on February 2.

Casualty figures during the battle that lasted from high summer to the abyss of the Russian winter are contradictory but the killed, wounded and missing at Stalingrad – subsequently renamed Volgograd – can be numbered in their hundreds of thousands.

Two at least lived in the sliver of No Man's Land between fact and fiction that is hope.